invincible

Cecily Anne Paterson

Published by Firewheel Books
www.cecilypaterson.com

ISBN: 978-0-9944975-1-2
© Cecily Anne Paterson 2014
Second edition 2014
Third edition 2015
Fourth edition 2020

Cover art by Emma Russell

This book is for every reader who has ever written
to tell me that Jazmine had an impact on their life.

chapter 1

The day after it all happens, I start to dream.

I'm not talking about, you know, *'follow your dreams'* or *'dream big and reach high'*, the sort of stuff people write on pictures of clouds and mountains or kittens tackling enormous balls of wool and then post all over the internet. I'm talking about proper, tucked-up-at-night dreams. Talking, fighting, travelling dreams. Dreams that pounce on you, drag you away by the hair, tie you to the bed and then jump on your chest until it hurts.

Nightmares.

You'd think after my dad had died, I would have dreamt about that. You'd think when we moved house, time and time again, I might have gone back to all the old places in my sleep. You'd think after the whole bullying thing at school I would have had some kind of material for my brain to play with after lights out.

But, no. I haven't dreamt — that is, had a dream I could remember in the morning — since Dad's funeral. For four years my mind has been blank and quiet. I've gone to bed, shut my eyes, tossed a little and then gotten up in the morning.

Until now.

Now, I'm making up for lost time. I'm a night passenger on a speed-seeking, haunted amusement ride. A different one every night. I wake in the dark, panting and exhausted, filled with terror or horror — whatever this night's particular ride specialises in.

Some nights people with no faces chase me through shopping malls and try to kill me.

Some nights monsters with green tails and black eyes oozing pus chase me through forests and try to kill me.

Some nights I'm walking with my friends; Gabby on one side, Liam on the other. I step behind for a minute, call them to notice an unusual tree with vivid blue leaves. When they turn back, their eyes are wild and they try to kill me.

The nights I get a break from all the killing and the death are the nights that I'm in the middle of a storm on a stony outcrop at the top of a mountain. The wind howls and the rain nearly knocks me over but I stand there at the top, looking at the storm clouds below. On those nights I know I've won, but the dream doesn't end there. It drags on and on while I clamber down the rock face, find my footing on mossy boulders and then slog my way through the muddy forest, filthy and wet until I see light in the trees.

I wake in the sunlight, sweaty, tired and just slightly out of breath.

When I get out of bed, the lino floor under my feet is surprisingly reassuring. There's a stickiness in each step, a tiny toe grip. As if my soles are clinging to what is solid. To what is warm. To what is real.

The morning after the first night it happens I tell it all to Mum. She's sitting, sleepy in her dressing gown, both hands hugging a cup of tea, an uneaten bowl of cereal on the table.

"...And then, it was like, I don't know, kind of like it was real, but it actually wasn't, if you know what I mean?" I say. "It's really hard to explain. And then the shark thing turned into a person and I just knew it was my complete enemy, even though I hadn't actually talked to it." I shake my head.

Mum opens her eyes wide. She makes a face like she's not sure. "It sounds really scary," she says. "Are you okay, Jazmine?" She signs it as well because my hearing aids aren't in and I'm lip reading. *You okay?*

"Yeah," I say. But I don't actually know if that's true because it's all so new and vivid. My body feels plugged in, slightly alive. Like someone's brushed my hair five hundred times, pricked my skin with a thousand pins and shone lights in my eyes.

Am I okay? I'm... something. I just don't know what.

At school I trail the remnants of the night's crazy adventures off the bus and into the playground before they are trodden on, pulled apart and ground into the dirt by a thousand uncaring feet. Liam has started waiting for me at the gate now so we can walk in together. Gabby's usually late but you don't miss her entrance. Today she's wearing a striped rainbow sock around her head. I know it's a sock rather than a headband because it has toes. They're dangling down by her ear.

"Do you *love* it?" she says, gesturing to her head. "Such a great idea, right?"

"Gabby, it's a sock," says Liam. "You're wearing hosiery on your head."

"Hosiery?" says Olivia, who's standing nearby.

Her identical twin, Caitlin, giggles. "Did you just use the word 'hosiery'?"

"My mum works at Myer," says Liam. He seems offended and I can't tell if he's just pretending. "I'm educated. I know all the different sections of a department store. Hosiery, manchester, millinery…"

Erin, sitting next to the twins, rolls her eyes and Liam's friend Dan groans. "Manchester? Millinery?"

"I think it's cute, Gab," I say. "It suits you."

"Ha. You see?" says Gabby triumphantly. "I can always count on you to have the *right* opinion," she says to me. "Unlike *some*." She glares at Liam, but it's not mean. Then she puts on a pose. "See? I'm starting a trend. By the end of today *everyone*," and she gestures around the school grounds, "will be wearing socks on their heads."

I smile at her. "You're funny."

She puckers her lips and pretends to blow me a kiss before she slaps Dan's hands away from the sock. He's trying to grab it off her head. "Get lost!" she bellows. "This is off limits. For my hands and my head only."

I watch her eyes, flashing with humour. Liam's the same. He's teasing Gabby, trying to de-sock her, but he's being funny. And friendly. It's a small kind of relief. Not that I think they really would kill me, but since the dreams began, there's been a question at the back of my brain.

Can I really trust them? Or, perhaps even more scary

for me: *Why would my subconscious even want to think up this stuff?*

Liam breaks into my thoughts. "Okay, so, I'll see you later? Are you going to the canteen at recess?"

"Um, no," I say. "Mum packed me a bacon and egg roll from home."

"Well I'll meet you outside C block then," he says. "You've got English, right? We can walk together."

I frown slightly. Some days I wouldn't mind just walking on my own. "Okay," I say, but it's more of a question.

He doesn't notice, and goes to leave. "I'll text you."

I pull my mouth sideways but nod anyway. My phone has become an issue. Before, when I was Little-Miss-No-Friends, I used it when I needed to, which was hardly ever. Now Mum's raising eyebrows whenever I ask for more credit, which is a lot. She pays, of course. I think she's terrified not to. For her, *Keeping Jazmine Happy And Sociable* is a thing. A big thing. A thing she's not going to muck up. Sometimes, I wonder if it will last, just like she probably does. And I'm not talking about the phone. I mean the happiness.

But there's no reason to think it's only going to be temporary. Since the drama production, either Liam or Gabby has been next to me the whole time, including after school. At school I'm part of their group. People know me. And text me.

From Gabby: *Hey, do you have any rainbow socks? Want to wear them tomorrow with me? Xxxx ooooo xxxxx*

From Liam: *You should come hang at my place this afternoon. We can walk home together.*

From Gabby: *Unbelievable! You're never going to guess what happened. Tell you at recess.*

I check my messages under my desk. My battery is running low, about six per cent. I forgot to charge it overnight. You're not actually supposed to have phones in class but everyone does. Most teachers ignore it but Miss Patel gets extra-stroppy and I don't need any hassles. At the very least I can try to save my mum from having to come see me in the Principal's office. After all the troubles ended last term she made me promise there'd be no more crises.

"Just tell me what's going on," she said when she came backstage to find me after the show was all over. She hugged me, still teary and emotional after the standing ovation and the post-production buzz. "That's all I want. I just need to know what's happening." Then she signed so only I could understand her: *Even if it's bad.*

"You too." I gripped her arms. "I never want to have any secrets ever again."

And so we began over again. Life, phase two. Things are simpler when you don't hide away.

Except, nightmares.

I breathe out hard when I think about them, slightly sick. They're not really something I can tell my friends about. *Hey guys, guess what? Last night I was chased by a creepy humanoid guy with a leather face and sunken eye sockets. He ambushed me in the shops and threatened to stick a knife in me the whole night until I woke up. The night before I was in a row boat in a crashing storm on a massive wave on an ocean that grew more mean, loud and scary by the second. Oh yeah, and on Tuesday you guys were all set to murder me.*

Soooo... d'ya think this is normal? Much?

I imagine Erin's eyes squinting slightly, her face turning away and then changing the subject. The twins would immediately come back with a detail-by-tiny-detail account of one of their (apparently combined) dreams from four years ago. Liam might ask a polite question or two but the other boys would raise their eyebrows, say something loud and brash and then act out sticking a knife in someone on the grass, with added gruesome bits.

Gabby... well, I don't know what Gabby would do.

Perhaps I'll take a chance and tell her. I'll just have to wait until she takes a breath between sentences because right now, even while eating her cheese and biscuits, Gabby is in full flight.

"You are seriously not going to believe what happened. I mean, I expected Angela to say something about it. She would, right? Made some comment in her posh voice... I don't even know what. But then Miss Eltham called me up. I mean, I couldn't believe it. She looked right at my head and she said, 'take that off Gabby,' just like that, with that exact strict voice... just 'Take That Off Gabby' and so I asked why, and she said, 'It's not school uniform'."

Gabby throws her bag on the grass with a flourish and takes another bite of cracker. Truly, she should go out for drama. She'd be amazing. I stand, waiting for her to continue. I don't have to wait very long.

"Then I said to Miss Eltham, just like this, in this voice, like, really nicely and everything, 'But Miss, we're allowed to wear accessories in our hair.' Honestly, I was so polite, but she just said, 'Gabby, it's a sock on your head'. I said, 'No Miss, it's a fashion statement,' and she said I had to take it off or I'd have to 'tell my fashion statement to the deputy'."

She makes a face, stuffs the rest of the cheese in her mouth and slumps on to the picnic bench.

"Oh, and of course snotty Angela was laughing at me so I just turned around and gave her my worst look. She's a ..." She turns her face away and her voice goes down to a low grumble that I can't pick up. She mouths something and I can't read her lips but I know what she's saying. Angela's been rubbing Gabby up the wrong way ever since last term, mostly because of her attitude to me because of the play and everything that happened. I just try to ignore it, but Gabby reacts really strongly.

"Did you take the sock off?" asks Olivia, worried.

"You don't want to go see Mr Barry," adds Caitlin. She looks genuinely scared.

Gabby wipes the crumbs from her face before pulling the rainbow sock out of her bag and jiggling it in front of the twins' faces. "I had no choice. I had to take it off. But I couldn't believe it. I mean, yeah sure, it's a sock, but it *becomes* a hairpiece if I wear it on my head, right? It's an accessory."

"I'm sorry for you," I say. I mean it. "It looked cute."

She makes a pouty face. "I know, right? It was going to take off. Next week everyone — even stupid Angela — would have had a sock on their head."

"You mean an accessory," I say and smile. I'm definitely getting better at making jokes.

She swats me with the sock. "Of course. An accessory."

There's a short silence. One of those times when the conversation is over but no one has started anything new yet. It's not normal for Gabby. She can talk and talk and talk. Sometimes I think she must have no secrets at all. Everything just pours out of her mouth. Maybe I should take a lesson from her. I sit up straighter and decide that yes, I'll talk about the dreams. I really will. I open my mouth, take in a breath and nearly begin but I'm interrupted. It's Liam. He's leaning over to me and tapping me on the knee so he can make sure I hear him.

"So, are you coming over?" he says. He's looking at me, intent. "This afternoon. I think you should."

I adjust my hearing aid slightly. His voice isn't as loud as Gabby's.

"I'll have to text Mum," I say. "But it should be okay."

"Good," he says. He smiles and his blue eyes knife my heart.

"Great." I grin back stupidly. "That would be great." The nightmares, all shapes and sizes, shuffle awkwardly into a back room in my brain where they bump up against each other, squashed and huddled. I shut the door and turn the key.

Later.

chapter 2

On the afternoons that I go to Liam's place after school, I let him hold my hand once we're far enough away from school that no one can see us. Today he takes me a different way.

"Where are we going?" I ask. "Don't we cross here?"

"You'll see," he says. He's mysterious and in control.

Just a little way down the road he pulls me into a small park. I've driven past it with Mum before but never stopped.

"Check this out," he says. "You like gardens, right?"

There in front of us is a large tree with spreading branches. But there are no leaves. Just a huge, glorious mass of tiny pink and white blossoms. It looks like a party dress.

"Oh!" I say. I can hardly get any words out. I walk towards it, stand underneath and look up. The blue spring sky twinkles in the tiny spaces between the flowers. I breathe in, long and deep. I recognise the smell but I can't remember where I've come across it before.

"Air sugar," I say, dreamily. "Is this a cherry blossom?"

Liam laughs. "Who cares what it is? I don't have a clue."

I reach up to a branch above my head and carefully pick a sprig of tiny flowers. "I'm going to go home and look it up," I say. I turn back to Liam but he's suddenly right next to me. "See how pretty they are?"

I hold out the flowers but he doesn't even look. Instead he grabs my waist and comes in close to my face.

"I don't care about the flowers," he says. "I'd rather look at something else."

He leans in and kisses me and all I can think is that this is probably the most romantic kiss I'll ever have, here, under this tent of colour and light. It's beautiful, and then it's not. It's awkward. I want to look up again and enjoy the place, to hold hands and maybe even dance a little but Liam is pressing his lips against mine, harder and longer. I try to break away and take a breath and he won't let me.

"Don't stop," he says, grabbing at my shirt and putting his hands right around to my back. His words are muffled.

I feel a slight panic rise in my stomach. I push him away firmly but try to laugh it off.

"Your mum's going to be wondering where we are," I say, lightly. I wipe my mouth with the back of my hand. "Maybe we should go."

"Is that all you're worried about?" he asks. He makes an 'it doesn't matter' face. "It's only Mum. If Dad was there I might be more fussed, but he's away. She doesn't count. We can do what we like." He steps back in and reaches out for me. "Come on."

I take his hands away from my waist and hold them instead. "I don't know," I say. And I'm embarrassed. It's not that I don't like kissing. I do. The first night of *The Secret Garden* production last term, that terrible night of truth and tears and laughter and flying happiness; that was the night that Liam first kissed me.

We danced off the stage, away from our standing ovation, with light feet, smiles of glitter and hearts with wings.

"Yeah, alright!" Liam high fived the cast waiting to congratulate him. "So awesome, everybody! Fantastic job." I followed behind; my face had no choice but to beam and grin. "Thanks, thank you," I said, over and over. Waves of faces and streams of words flowed over and around me. There were suddenly so many people, so much noise and so many bright lights. The smile stayed on my face but underneath I was scared. My smile was pasted on; my eyes were fearful. Perhaps it was everything I'd been through that day, perhaps I was tired, or perhaps I wasn't cut out to be a celebrated actress. Whatever it was, I felt dizzy. Zoned out. Breathless.

Liam turned in the crowd and the chatter. He must have seen my face go pale because he grabbed my wrist and pulled me behind him.

"Jaz needs to sit down." His voice crawled through the tunnels of cloud into my brain. He must have been speaking loudly. Forcefully. "Out of the way you guys. I'm going to take her in there."

He pushed me into the dressing room, empty except for some costumes on the floor and a few chairs pulled up next to a mirror. I collapsed onto one of them and folded my head in my hands.

"Sorry," I said. He was crouched down next to me, his hand on my back.

"What for?" he said. "I could see you weren't okay. Just breathe a bit."

"Oh, I mean, okay," I said. But he cut in.

"And stop talking. Just take a breath."

I stopped talking and instead took air into my lungs. Outside I could hear the buzz of voices and loud laughter but it was like there was a cocoon of cotton around the room. Our room. I focused on the breathing. *Air in. Air out. Air in. Air out.* My shoulders relaxed a little. I looked up.

"Thanks," I said. "I don't know... I just felt so..."

"Crowded?" he said. He smiled at me and pulled up one of the other chairs so he was sitting opposite. "You looked like you were about to faint. I thought I'd better rescue you."

I smiled weakly.

"Do you feel better now?"

I shook my arms and blinked a few times. "Yeah. I think so. I just felt like I couldn't..."

But I didn't get a chance to say anything else. Liam pulled his chair up so his knees were touching mine. And then he put out his hand to turn my face towards his. It sucked the breath out of me. My heart started pounding and my head went dizzy again, but this time in a good way.

"Are you..." I began, but again, I didn't get a chance to speak because in one swift movement Liam reached in and kissed me. Right on the lips.

It was a short kiss (and really, I'm only judging it on the movie kisses I've seen, so maybe that's not realistic anyway) but it felt like forever. And then, the afterwards, with him looking into my eyes, his hand still on my cheek and the tingle of softness still on my mouth, felt like forever all over again.

I managed to get my words out this time. Well, my one word out, anyway.

"Wow."

Liam just sat and looked at me. He put his hand down on his lap. For once, he seemed almost tongue-tied.

"You," he said and he nodded his head slightly. "You. Just. Are." He shrugged. "Amazing."

My joy came scrambling out from its hiding place. It filled my skin, danced in my eyes and tingled in my fingers. Even my hair felt alive. I blushed. "Really?"

Liam grinned. He was back to his usual self. "Yeah. Really."

I gazed at him. I could hardly trust myself to speak. If I opened my mouth who knew what would come out? That I thought he was the most beautiful boy in the whole entire world? That I would do anything for him? That I couldn't stop looking at him, or thinking about him?

I held it back and instead squeaked words which didn't even begin to say what the truth of it was. Stupid words. Words I could hardly push out of my mouth for fear of not being right, not being good enough. I said to Liam, the boy who had rescued me twice that evening, and who had just kissed me and called me 'amazing': "I like you."

Yeah. Good job, Jazmine.

He looked at me seriously. His blue eyes were piercing. "I will always be there to look after you, you know. Before you even know you need me, I'll be there."

Perhaps it was at that point that I should have listened to the slight warning bell that went off in the back corner of my brain, but I was too full of amazing and kisses and tingly glittery happiness to pay any attention to it. Instead I told it to go away. *Leave me and my happiness alone.*

That was the first time. After that it became a kiss goodbye at the end of the afternoon. Recently, though, it's turned into all of *this*; this touching, grasping, serious lip-locking, or at least serious attempts at it, on Liam's part.

Perhaps I'm just immature, just babyish, but it feels like too much somehow, like I'm belting down rapids in a river in a canoe that already has a hole in it. I'm slightly out of control and I have this nagging fear that the whole thing's going to capsize before I get the hang of it. I'm confused. Is it possible that maybe I just don't want to move this fast? Is that normal?

If I had it my way, I'd have more picnics in the sunshine, more patting puppies and more early evening bike rides. I'd do more talking and more gazing, more sharing of sunsets. I'd quite like poetry. And flowers.

You know. Romance.

But that's hard to say. Especially when he's back in my face and I have to move his hands. Again.

"What's the matter?" he asks. "Don't you like me anymore?"

"No, that's not it at all," I say. But he looks almost angry, which makes me worried.

"Well, that's what you're acting like," he says. "I didn't think you'd be like that. Not after all this time." He walks off and plants himself on the park bench, arms crossed and legs out wide. I follow him over and sit nervously on the edge.

"Like what?" I say.

"Like the girls who say one thing but act another way." He kicks at the grass. "I thought you were honest."

"I am," I say, slightly confused.

"Well, if you really were into me like you say you are, then you wouldn't have a problem with what we're doing. Plus we've been going out for weeks now," he says. He turns to me. "So all I can think is that maybe you don't like me. Maybe you want to break up."

A flash of terror floods my heart. "No!" I say. It's almost a yelp. "No. I really, really like you. I don't want to break up. Please don't say that." Above me the blue sky seems to be turning to grey.

"Well, you have to prove it, you know," he says. "Otherwise it's just words."

"I will," I say, wildly. I move in close to him and reach for his hand. "See?"

"It's weird. It's kind of out of my control but I just can't help liking you," he says but he pulls his hand away from mine. I shrink back. My hand looks alone there on the painted green palings of the park bench. "I mean, it's true, most people don't see what I see in you, but I just think you're so amazing."

He looks in my eyes. His are big, wide, innocent, searching. I can see truth. And love. I melt and the panic goes away.

"You're so beautiful, Jazmine," he says. "I want to treat you like a princess." He touches my cheek gently. "But you have to do your part too."

I nod. It's all I can do. I've gone from terrified, cast out and torn off to safe and loved again, all in the space of two minutes.

He smiles at me kindly and shakes his head. "Maybe you should just go home," he says. "That's probably the best thing for now." He stands up to go. "I'll see you tomorrow. Meet you at the gate."

I nod again, scrabble around for my bag and go to leave. There's a slight breeze and from the corner of my eye I see pink and white blossoms floating gently off the tree and onto the ground. I look down and move my foot when I see I'm treading on them, turning them into a brown mash and grinding them into the grass.

I walk away, but I keep looking back until I can't see Liam any more.

chapter 3

My mind is anxious and my feet are tired when I finally make it home. I'm surprised that Mum's car isn't in the driveway yet. Her work day finishes just after the school bell goes and she's been back home at the same time as me, or just a little later, practically every afternoon of my life.

All I want to do is collapse on my bed and pretend the thing at the park with Liam never happened.

Massive fail.

There must be something wrong with me. I mean, Liam is like, the perfect boy. The perfect boyfriend. Maybe he's right. I'm not being honest. I'm not showing him I like him. I just didn't realise it would feel so scary. And confusing. For some reason I thought love would be simpler than it's turning out to be.

I go through my bag for the front door key but it's not there. *Of course!* When Mum washed my bag on the weekend in a lets-clean-everything-up frenzy, she took the key out. I was supposed to put it back in again once it was dry.

Double massive fail.

I sit miserably on the steps for a minute. All I want to do is find out if Liam's still angry with me. I pull my phone out and press the button to turn it on but it beeps once and the screen goes black. *Batteries!* I think in disgust and shove it back in with the books. There's nothing to do except wait.

But then I remember. I left the side gate unlocked this morning. And there's definitely something to do in the backyard. Weeds are crawling into my garden beds, spreading and taking up space that should belong to the spring flower seeds I planted a few weeks ago. I've known for days I have to do something about them but every afternoon I've been with either Gabby or Liam and the hours have disappeared quicker than the daylight.

The gate squeaks as I let myself in and tread the old, uneven concrete path down to the back. In the beds, green shoots are growing. I throw my bag on the back steps, pick up my trowel and squat down at the edge of the soil. The smell of earth fills my body; my shoulders are lighter. I dig at the tough kikuyu grass that's come in from the neighbour's lawn, under the fence and popped up next to my seedlings.

Annoying.

My worries disappear into the garden. Perhaps it's the *doing* of it, the pulling, touching, tending, planning, caring. Perhaps it's the sun on my back, the air on my face, the light in my eyes. In my garden I focus on one thing only: giving my plants the best chance to grow. Flower. Flourish.

Time disappears too. Before I know it there's a car in the driveway and Mum in the kitchen. I wipe my hands on my school uniform and knock at the back door.

"You?" says Mum, holding it open, two seconds later. Her face is surprised. Perhaps slightly guilty? I can't figure out why that would be the case so I push the thought away. "Didn't you say you were going to Liam's?"

"Came home early." I shrug my shoulders. "Stuff."

I walk past her through the laundry and into the small kitchen. "Is there anything to eat?"

"There are still some bananas left," she says. "Or you could make a sandwich." Her voice changes. I can hear the slight anxiety. "Anything wrong? Is Liam okay?"

I pause in front of the fruit bowl, my back turned. There's a beat before I reply. "No. It's all good. He just had to go a bit earlier. His mum wanted..." I let my voice trail off. For a tiny moment I had considered telling her about the kissing and the canoe in the rapids feeling and the fact that I'm not normal because I don't want to go so fast. But just as quickly, a flush of something like embarrassment shuts the whole thing down.

You can't say that to your mum. How totally, overwhelmingly mortifying. You'd never be able to look at her ever again. Plus, are you going to admit you're a freak?

No, I decide. No, I am not. I will find a way to deal with this. Myself.

I take my banana, peel it, turn around. Change the subject. "Are you later than normal?"

There's an immediate pause. Something passes through Mum's eyes but I can't quite tell what it is. She twists her mouth. "Yeah, I'm a little later," she says. "Stuff." She smiles at me.

"Are you busy at the moment?" I ask.

"You could say that."

"Working back?"

"A little. It's kind of the beginning of a project. But I'll tell you about it when I know a bit more." She heads to the fridge. "Now I'm hungry. Think I'll make myself a sandwich."

"I should probably do my homework," I say. "Before dinner." Mum nods and I head to my room. Homework's not really at the top of my list though. I may have stretched the truth with that one. Charging my phone is going to come first.

I plug it in and wait until the battery chime goes. Then I unpack my bag, arrange my books on my desk and pull out a pen. And my journal.

I breathe.

And open it. I flip through the pages until I find the next empty one. It's cream and clean and smooth. And simple.

Unlike my thoughts.

I take my pen and begin, not to write, but to draw. Words are clogging up my head. For some reason I can't trust them today. So I use pictures instead.

I'm not a good artist, but here, now, today, on this page, it doesn't matter. I want to draw that tree, those blossoms. I want to remember the colour and the scent and the sparkle of the sky in a clean, clear, smooth way. I don't want the ugly mess at the end, the confusion and tears. I want the beauty, the freedom, the power of an incredible tree on an incredible day.

I draw for a long time, and then dig through my drawers for some pencils and crayons to shade it with.

When I'm finished, I sit back and look at it. And then I draw myself, a tiny stick figure, standing next to Liam, a second tiny stick figure, under the spreading branches. Just standing together. That's all.

There's a beep from my phone. The batteries are at 20 per cent. Definitely useable now. I grab it off its cord, flick through to the messages and scroll down looking for Liam's name. There it is, on the text he sent me inviting me to his place this afternoon. I press 'Reply' and sit on the bed, thinking. How do you say what I need to say? *Do you still like me? Do you know I didn't mean it? That all I want to do is be with you?* I type some words.

Hey Liam, Are you…

Hi. Hey, you know…

I really do like…

But it all looks wrong. I delete, erase, extinguish sentence after sentence. It's too hard. I lay back on the bed, the phone thrown down beside me. Perhaps I'll just leave it. Perhaps I'll just wait until tomorrow. Pretend nothing happened. Just keep going like everything's normal.

Yeah.

Normal.

As if I even know what that is.

Suddenly I'm tired. It's not the walking or the gardening or even the schoolwork. It's something else and I can't put my finger on it. I feel too exhausted to even think about texting Liam. He'll just have to wait.

I push my phone away but as I do it buzzes. I pick it up anyway. Force of habit. It's from Gabby. I flip over so I'm lying on my stomach and read her message.

Socks are yesterday's thing. Tomorrow it's going to be wombats. Wait and see! PS. Have you done your science assignment yet? I'm stuck on question 5. HELP ME!!!!!!!

My tiredness sits back for a bit and a smile that I can't help comes over my face. Boys are confusing. Best friends, on the other hand, are totally, completely reliable.

chapter 4

When I finally get to bed, I get a reprieve from the nightly horror movie in my head. I still dream. But it's not scary and I don't wake up flustered and sweating. What I do wake up with, though, is a picture of someone. A picture I can't get rid of. A picture I haven't seen for a long, long time.

It's my grandma.

After four years with no contact — visits, phone calls, even birthday cards — I'm amazed that (a) Grandma popped up in my head, completely unannounced, and (b) that I even recognised her. Dreams are the funniest things though. I haven't thought about Grandma for all that time but at 3am, asleep in my bed, I can even remember the name and the scent of her perfume.

Plum blossom. Like the tree. It's sweet, musky. Even a little tangy.

Pictures and memories pour in, all in an instant and I'm holding her hand and touching her long nails, always some shade of bright pink or orange; playing next to the roses while she prunes in her rose-print gardening gloves; trying on her necklaces, chunky and colourful. A thought pops into my head. It grows in an instant to fill the room and then I'm alive with the possibilities.

We've got to visit Grandma.

But, *oh.*

The pictures fall away, the excitement dissolves and it's just me again, in my room, standing in blue monkey pyjamas next to a pile of dirty clothes on a cloudy Thursday morning.

Mum.

She doesn't have to say it, but I know anyway. She's angry with Grandma. She's been angry since the funeral. Since the big family talk after it. Since we moved. That's why she sent back cards and didn't take calls. *She won't do you any good,* she told me when I asked. Who knows? Maybe she was angry before Dad's suicide. Maybe she and Grandma never got on. In-laws don't sometimes. I don't know. She doesn't talk about it. All I know is that every time I've asked, the answer has been 'no'. But you can't say no forever, right?

I go out to the kitchen for breakfast. Mum's there already. She's made her tea; the cereal's out on the bench and she's checking her email on her phone.

"Hey," I say.

She jumps a little, looks up and quickly swipes her phone screen so the emails have gone.

"Jaz, I didn't hear you." She smiles. A little too wide for this time of the morning. "Sleep well?"

I take a breath to steady me. "Yeah. Good, thanks."

"No bad dreams?"

"No. Not bad ones," I say, slowly. I narrow my eyes slightly. I'll have to face it sometime. It might as well be now. "Really weird ones though."

She tilts her head and sips her tea, waiting for me to continue.

"Yeah. I mean, so weird. You won't believe it. I actually dreamt about Grandma."

I watch Mum's face as I say her name. There's a slight flinch there, a small flicker of her eyes, twitch of her mouth.

"Really?" she says. It sounds a little strained. Or maybe I'm reading too much into it. It's hard to know. I carry on, regardless. Reckless.

"It was so real. We were just, like, in the garden together, having a normal kind of chat about school."

"Hmdghmgf," says Mum, taking a bite of her cereal. It's one of those all-purpose mouth noises that means nothing and everything all at the same time.

I turn around so I'm deliberately not looking at her when I go to ask the all-important question. I don't want to see her face if she says no.

"So. It got me thinking. I'd like to visit Grandma sometime. You know. Go back. It's been, like, years."

Behind me, there is either a long silence or my hearing aids aren't turned up enough and I've totally missed Mum's reply.

Awkward.

I grab the bread out of the fridge and turn around again. "I said I'd quite like to visit Grandma."

Mum's facing the sink. She's sort of gripping it with her fingers. Which look white.

"I'll have to think about it, Jaz," she says, still turned away from me. Her voice is small. Faraway. "It's not something I can answer straight away. Especially not at breakfast."

She fumbles with the dishes, clean in the rack. I can see her phone poking out of her pocket. She throws the cutlery, clinking and clanking, into the drawer and then crashes the plates into the cupboard. I feel the tension in the room, decide that toast doesn't matter and go back to my room with unbuttered bread. It'll do. Later I'll buy a hot chocolate at the canteen. Maybe an apple as well. But right now I'll just get dressed and go to school.

Which turns out to be a pretty good plan, actually. I have to walk because I'm way too early for the bus and I get to the school gate before it even arrives. In fact, I'm there before most people have arrived. There's a Year 7 kid spread out on the concrete playing his iPod and some Year 11 girls bunched in a tight group exclaiming over something, but the path, usually buzzing with energy and full of people, is clear. Empty. Almost peaceful.

And, something else.

Liam isn't at the gate.

I'm surprised at how much lighter I feel when I see he's not there. Like I can breathe. Like my bag weighs less. Which is stupid, I know. I mean, I *like* that he meets me here every day. I *like* that we walk down the path together. I like *him*.

Today, though, it's just one less thing to think about. Maybe if I manage to stick with Gabby or the twins and Erin most of the day I'll avoid the potentially awkward conversations. Maybe we'll be able to just hang out comfortably. Like we used to.

I sit on our usual picnic table and watch the school fill up in front of me. It's like one of those time lapse photography things they do in nature docos. The quadrangle goes from being a concrete desert to a hustling, scurrying jungle in half an hour. It brings a smile to my face. I used to arrive at school and try to hide. It was just all too much for me. These days I feel like I'm okay. At least mostly. I've got friends I hang with, I'm polite to everyone else and I seem to manage okay, as long as no one gets in my face, especially not Angela and her crowd, who still seem to have something against me from when the drama production was on.

Dan's the first of our group to arrive, followed by Erin and the twins. They throw their bags down and say hi.

"You're early," says Dan, looking confused.

"I walked," I say.

"All that way?" gasps Olivia.

"Don't your feet hurt?" asks Caitlin.

"It's not that far," I say.

"Where's Liam?" asks Dan. He cranes his head to see behind me, as if I'm hiding him somewhere.

I shrug. "Not here yet."

"Is Gabby going to wear that sock again today?" asks Erin. She shakes her head. "She's nuts."

"She's funny," I say. "But no. She texted me. Something about wombats."

"Wombats?" Caitlin and Olivia say it together and in exactly the same high-pitched tone.

Identicals, I grin to myself. It's what Gabby started calling them after they turned up at a sleepover at her place in the holidays with matching pyjamas and teddy bears. When I first met them I had to wait until they were smiling to be able to tell them apart. Olivia has a tiny gap in her front teeth but Caitlin's teeth are perfectly straight and even. But they really are as identical as identical twins can be. Thankfully I don't have to wait until their mouths are open to figure out who is who because at the moment they have slightly different haircuts. Olivia's is down to the middle of her back while Caitlin's sits an inch below her shoulders. Sometimes she even wears it up, but always with a ribbon.

Thinking of ribbons reminds me of socks… I squint into the distance. There's Gabby, walking up in the way that only she can do. Confident. *I own the world.* It looks like she's brought her dog. To school? Surely not. But it's brown. And furry. And it's on a leash. I blink a few times.

"Is that a wombat?" I ask. Erin and the twins turn to look too.

"No. Wombats are bigger than that," says Erin. "We had one under our house once. It was huge."

More kids in the quad are starting to look now. I can practically see Angela's eye-roll from here. Her friends are looking at each other, like, *what is going on there?* Across the way, a group of boys from my Science class are following Gabby's progress up the path. One, a messy-haired, taller boy, laughs and points, but not in a mean way.

Gabby sees us looking. She waves. And then she begins to run. The whatever-it-is is dangling wildly from the end of the leash which seems firm now, rather than rope-like. A little like a fishing rod, maybe? The twins scream. Together, of course.

"Gabby! Don't!"

But Gabby keeps going, completely ignoring the animal being tossed around. I put my hands to my mouth and hold my breath.

"Don't be stupid, you guys," says Dan. "It's stuffed."

"Are you kidding me?" yells Olivia. She hits Dan on the arm. "I thought it was real."

"I thought it was going to die," says Caitlin. She sits heavily on the bench and takes a deep breath.

Gabby arrives with a burst, breathless and smiling. "I just have to show you. Look. It's my pet wombat."

She holds out a stuffed, brown furry toy which is neither strangled nor dead. In fact, it looks pretty good. Very wombatish. And with a red ribbon around its neck.

"What *is* this?" I ask. I'm smiling because I can't help smiling when Gabby's around. I shake my head like I can't believe it. "A *wombat?*"

"It's cute," she says, pouting slightly. She perks up again. "I just thought it would be funny to bring him to school. His name's Wally." She grabs him around the belly and snuggles him up to her face.

"Wally the Wombat?" says Dan. "Real original Gabby."

"I don't see you bringing your wombat to school, Mr I'm-So-Original." She throws him a look that's half smiling, half mock-offended. "I'll let you pat him. But only if you're nice."

Dan holds his hands out. "I'll be nice," he says, but as soon as Gabby hands Wally over Dan gives him a kick out into the grass.

"No way!" yells Gabby and she pushes Dan over and

runs to retrieve Wally. She's slightly too late though. Liam has picked him up.

"Is this your wombat?" he says, bowing and holding it out.

"Thank you!" says Gabby with a big roll of the eyes towards Dan. She walks back to the seat, fussing over Wally and brushing dry bits of grass off him. Liam watches Gabby's dramatics with amusement, raising his eyebrows slightly. Then he slides in close, next to me on the seat.

"Hey," he says.

My heart is pounding slightly but I keep it together and put on a smile for him. Not too much, but more than just polite. "Hey," I say. "How are you?"

"You weren't on the bus," he says. "I was waiting for you at the gate."

"Oh." I say. "Sorry about that." I sound confused. "Um. I walked today."

"What time?" he says. "It must have been early. I've been at the gate for like 30 minutes. By myself." He seems hurt. "You could at least have called me or texted me or something."

I feel slightly guilty. He's right. I should have told him I wouldn't be there at the normal time. "Sorry," I say. "I didn't really think."

"What were you doing?" he asks. He moves back from me, still upset.

"Just sitting here," I say. I lean towards him a little, just so the space between us isn't so big. "Watching everyone."

"Who?" he says. It's a quick, strong question. *Bam.* I'm slightly taken aback.

"No-one," I say. "Just, you know," I shrug. "All the people coming in."

He looks around the quadrangle. There are groups of kids, all sizes, sitting and standing; chatting and playing handball. I can see the messy-haired boy and his friends from my Science class, shirts tucked out, exclaiming over some kind of comic book. Standing away from them are Angela and her blonde clones, the girls I try to avoid. They look mean, skirts hiked up, all cake-faced and wearing exactly the same hairstyle. Then there are the rest; big kids, smaller ones, pairs and groups from other years I've never even met. Liam's eyes scan it all. He's looking for something, but I'm not sure what.

And then his eyes stop on a group of Year 10 boys.

He frowns and opens his mouth to say something and I'm horrified because it's occurred to me that maybe he thinks I was watching them, muscular and laughing and kicking their footy around. I look back at him. His face, which is normally relaxed and happy seems tight and pinched. His hands are clenching up, just slightly, not that anyone else would notice, but I recognise it as the same reaction he gave his mum that one time that she asked him to take out the rubbish.

He did it. But he wasn't happy.

He's not happy now. And my heart is stretching inside my chest. It feels like fear, but it couldn't be. I mean, I'm not scared of Liam. Why should I be?

I just really don't like it when he's mad at me.

chapter 5

The first lesson of the day is drama. Gabby and I are back with Miss Fraser this term again. The person who changed my life. I'm pleased, obviously. But it is strange to now not be getting all of her attention. We must have spent four hours every day together for most of last term, what with practices and fittings and meetings about the play. Now she's just a regular teacher.

A nice one, yeah. But just a regular one.

And I am just a regular student again.

Which is weird.

I can't really tell Gabby how I feel. She's not really a person who enjoys hanging out with teachers, no matter who they are. For her, teachers are only there to torture her with pointless work she doesn't understand, to make her tone down her creative efforts at making people laugh and to tell her to keep her voice down. Constantly.

Because apparently she's loud. Like, really loud. Like, all the time. It's good for me. I never have to lip read or ask her what she said. Maybe it's not so good for class management, but I'm not a teacher, so I don't have to worry.

It's not just teachers who tell her to be quiet. Angela is sitting in front of us today and she's in a mood. I just take it as a given that she hates me, I guess because I was given her part in the play in the end, but I always just try to avoid her and hope she'll forget about it eventually. Now, for some reason she's got something against Gabby too. She's already given her about five dirties since we walked into class. I'll admit it. If you didn't 'get' the whole wombat thing, Gabby could possibly come across as annoying today. She has Wally on her lap and is patting it, cooing to it and making it into her pet.

Angela turns around.

"What is that thing?" she says. "Are you bringing your teddies to preschool now?"

Britney and Katie giggle next to her. They are pretty much carbon copies of Angela. They roll their eyes at Gabby and shake their hair over their shoulders. I can feel a blush rising up my neck at being singled out, but Gabby just laughs.

"It's 'bring a pet day' today, Angela. Didn't you know?" she says. "Oh, hang on — you did bring one — it's Britney."

Britney makes a face at her and turns away. Angela makes a frustrated noise, huffs and stalks over to the other side of the room with her friends where they stand whispering to each other. I can't hear them but I don't need to. I know they're hating on Gabby and probably me too.

I pass a note to Gabby. *Are you okay?*

She scribbles back a quick reply. *Why wouldn't I be?* And looks at me with genuine curiosity on her face.

Well, you know… I gesture with my head towards Angela and make a worried face.

"Her?" Gabby yelps. It's seriously loud. I look around anxiously, hoping nobody has noticed.

"I don't care what she thinks." She laughs. "She can't even touch me."

But she's mean, I write. I'm nervous about everyone listening. Gabby raises her eyebrows. "You've just got to surprise her," she says. "That's all it is. She's a bully. So get her before she gets you." She shrugs. "I've dealt with people like her before. It's no issue."

Gabby's confidence isn't comforting. It's hard to ignore the curious looks of everyone else sitting around us. The more friends I have, the more I'm seeing—all around me—that everyone loves it when other people fight. Even just last week Erin was buzzing with news about a massive argument between Sophie and Phoebe, two girls from my roll call class.

"Phoebe totally dissed her on Facebook. Plus she took a screen shot of an old conversation they had about who she liked and then sent it to the guy she was talking about," she said.

"Who was it?" asked Dan.

"This guy at Morton High," said Erin. 'Full of glee' were the only words I could think of to describe what her face looked like. "I think they catch the same bus. And now half the girls who sit on the benches are on Sophie's side, but most of the guys are with Phoebe because they reckon Sophie had it coming to her."

"You don't even talk to Sophie," said Gabby to Dan. "Why do you care?"

He shrugged. "I just like to know what's going on," he said.

I told Mum about it when I got home that night. She shook her head. "Why can't everyone just keep their heads out of everyone else's business?"

Gabby might be confident but I'm not. I can see a fight looming. We're going to get out of drama and all of our Year is going to be talking about how Gabby called Britney an animal. I can see people already getting their phones out under their desks. Quietly, so Miss Fraser won't notice.

You don't need guns to start a war. A mobile phone will do.

My stomach is churning while Gabby looks totally unconcerned. She even whistles in class until Miss Fraser tells her to stop.

Angela and her friends sit sulking with the newly-made-up besties Sophie and Phoebe, darting evil looks at us through recess and lunch. But nothing else happens. My fears are for nothing. At least for now.

I breathe a little sigh of relief as I walk to the front gate with Liam and Gabby as the final bell goes. Perhaps it will all die down. Everyone might have forgotten about it by tomorrow. Even Liam seems to be over his sulks. He's light-hearted again, running ahead with Dan and looking back at me and laughing as he tries to grab Dan's phone out of his hand. I grin and share the joke. I'm glad he's in a good mood with me. *One less thing to worry about.* A random thought occurs to me. Maybe I'm dreaming and having nightmares because I'm too anxious? I'll have to look that up on the net.

Dear Dr Google. Do I have nightmares because I'm stressed at school?

Later. Maybe. Because this afternoon I'm going to Gabby's place. Where there are never any worries.

Her mum is always there whenever we bang through the front door. Gabby drops her bag and kicks off her shoes immediately, yelling hello. I'm always more cautious, but it's only because of habit.

"Hi Mrs Smeeton," I say, tiptoeing around the corner to where she's pulling apart a chicken. I try to push down the shudder at the sight of raw meat. Dinner, I suppose. I wouldn't really know. My mum cooks things from packets.

"Hi girls," she says with a smile nearly as big as Gabby's. "Jazmine, would you please just call me Ann? You make me feel like my mother-in-law when you say Mrs Smeeton."

I grin, embarrassed. "Sorry," I say, but my mouth won't let me add the 'Ann'. It seems too personal. Too close.

Gabby launches herself up to the bar stool and looks around with hungry eyes. "There must be food, right?" she says. Her mum raises her eyebrows and Gabby gives an exasperated gasp. "Please, then."

"Yes, dear," says Call-Me-Ann. "We have food." She says it pointedly, to make a thing about Gabby forgetting her manners, but not like she's really cross. "I made croissants."

"Oh yeah," sings Gabby doing a happy dance. The bar stool is wobbling on its base. "Jaz. You have to taste these."

Gabby's mum pulls out a tray of — honestly, I am not joking — fresh, steaming croissants that look like they should be on the shelf of a bakery. A classy one. My mouth actually waters. Which is rare.

"Did you make them yourself?" I ask. I'm amazed. "Are they hard? How did you get time? After work?"

Ann laughs. "Oh, no," she says. "I don't have a job. A couple of times when we've moved I've been able to find some work, but it doesn't always happen that way. This time I haven't really bothered. Maybe in the next place."

A small switch goes off in my head. I'm immediately curious and open my mouth to ask a question but it doesn't even get out of my mouth. I am loudly, doggedly interrupted by Gabby. "Mum," she says. "Don't."

Her mum looks hurt. "I was only saying that — " she begins but Gabby speaks over her.

"Well don't even start," she says. "Come on Jaz. We'll eat them in my room."

Gabby's room is a mish-mash of over-stuffed cushions, pop posters and books spilling out of two shelves, with piles of extras on the floor. She has stuff. Lots of it. Every time I come I try to act like, *hey this is normal for me too*, but you can't compare the cupboard of a girl like Gabby with me. She spends Christmas with 15 different aunts, uncles and assorted cousins and her parents don't think twice before buying her the latest iPad or gadget any time of year. Me? I get two small gifts from one person — my mum — at Christmas and maybe three, if I'm lucky, on my birthday.

The fact is, when your mum works a basic reception job and there are only two of you and rent that has to be paid and you don't ever see your relatives because some time in the ancient past someone argued with someone else and couldn't—or wouldn't—make up, you simply don't have as much stuff as other people.

I always thought I was okay with that. Before. When I didn't know people. When I didn't know that maybe I could have a friend some day. Today, as I look at Gabby's pictures and listen to her music and eat her home-made croissants which taste like buttery bliss, I miss my life.

I mean, I miss what my life could have been.

I especially miss my grandma.

"I asked Mum if l could go visit my Dad's mother. My grandma," I say to Gabby who is licking every single one of her fingers in turn. She looks up at me with a puzzled face.

"I didn't know you had one," she says. "Grandma, I mean." She picks up the last croissant. "Do you want this?"

I shake my head and point to an uneaten half still on my lap. "Of course I have a grandma," I say.

"Where does she live?" asks Gab.

"I think it's Moruya," I say. "Some town on the South Coast."

When I look up, Gabby's face has turned as white as her freshly painted walls. Her mouth is tight and her eyes seem pained.

"What's the matter?" I ask. "You okay?"

She nods, miserable for a half second. Then she flashes her regular Gabby smile at me and looks around for Wally. "I think he's hungry," she says. "He definitely wants something to eat. Maybe I should go and ask Mum for more." She bounces off the bed and heads towards the door.

That switch goes off in my head again when she mentions her mum. It comes with a command. H*ey, ask that question again.*

So I ask it. Straight out. No faffing around.

"Hey Gab. When your mum said 'next time' did that mean that you're going to move again?"

Gabby stops. Her hand, reaching out for the doorknob, is frozen. There's just a tiny twitch in the back of her neck. Then, slowly, she turns to look at me. She takes a deep breath. And she talks.

"What are you on about? What a stupid subject. Plus," and here she looks down at Wally, cradled in her other arm, "you are depriving a very hungry wombat from eating his dinner." She brings out her cheeky face. "Wally won't be your friend if you don't let him eat."

I make a mock sorry face to Wally and watch Gabby leave the room, yelling for her mum. I flop back onto her bed and my eyes go straight to a poster of Gabby's favourite boy band pinned to the ceiling. Cameron Ellis, the cute, charming one of the group with the best voice looks a little like Liam, I decide. Except I can't imagine *him* getting mad, he's so gorgeous. I examine all of their faces and the different colours of their messy, tousled hair and I forget all about Gabby's plans or not-plans to move on.

chapter 6

There's something up with Mum. I can tell the second I walk through the kitchen door. Her usual cup of tea is on the table, but she's sitting straighter than normal. She looks jumpy.

"Hi," I say. Carefully. And then, "you okay?"

She beams a very large smile at me. It's the sort of smile they put on in ads for painkillers. *Look! My back doesn't hurt any more!*

"You're going," she says.

I narrow my eyes slightly. I'm puzzled.

"You're going," she says again. "In the holidays."

I tip my head to one side. "I'm sorry. What?"

The smile hasn't let up. "You're going to her place. Your grandma. In the holidays."

"Woah. Are you kidding?" I drop my bag and my jaw meets it on the floor.

"No." Mum's face goes a little more normal when she starts to talk. "After this morning I thought to myself, *you know, she's right.* There's no reason you shouldn't see your grandmother just because she and I had an argument. Especially now you're older." She sips her tea and brushes something off her nose. "So I rang her and you're going for the school holidays."

I fiddle with my hearing aid. "What?"

"Say pardon, Jaz. It's more polite," says Mum. She's looking away from me. She hasn't noticed that I'm still standing in the same spot, too shocked to move.

"But the holidays are in, like, a week. Ten days away." I stop talking. I don't need to give Mum reasons for me to stay home. I change tack. "Are you sure?" I say. "And do you mean the whole holidays? The full fortnight?" I'm pinching myself. Surely I've misheard.

"It'll give me a chance to sort a few things out," she says. And then adds, "Things at work. Work things." She turns to the sink. I can't see her face. "It's getting pretty full-on at the moment. Lots to do."

Odd. I've never seen Mum show more than the barest amount of enthusiasm for her job. But, whatever. I need to get a straight answer to the most important question. "How long am I staying for?" I ask.

"The whole holidays. Grandma insisted."

"So you actually spoke to her?" My voice goes high. Excited. "Today?"

"When do you think it was?" Mum turns around. She has her 'silly Jazmine' face on. She uses it to tease me. "It's only this morning you mentioned it, right? It's not like I'm some guru prophet person who can see into the future and organise stuff before you've even thought of it."

I shake my head. *I can't believe it*, I sign. I'm saying it to Mum, obviously. But I'm really saying it to myself, to my absent-for-four-years Grandma and to my Dad.

I wonder if he ever thought about what would and wouldn't happen after he died. *I can't believe it.*

Well, it's true, signs Mum. *So I hope you two will get along.*

There's a hint of snark. Just a tiny one. But I bite my tongue. No point fighting about this, a thing we haven't talked about for years, even in our post-landmark-event/brand-new-life-of-Jazmine era because we both know it will end with her tight-lipped and me sulking, holed up my room, only coming out to eat and drink and go to the bathroom.

No. *Be thankful for what you've got,* I tell myself. I decide to smile. "Mum. Thanks. I really... well, just... thanks."

She smiles too. "I think it will work out well for both of us."

I look at her for a second, my eyes narrowed. And then I leave it. *Not worth it, whatever it is,* I think. And I pick up my bag.

"Is there time for me to go out to the garden before dinner?" I ask.

"Oh," she says. "Dinner's not even close. I haven't given a single thought about what to have. I'm not that hungry. You?"

I shrug. "I don't mind. Had something at Gabby's." I throw my stuff in my room and head outside to the garden.

The spring evening air is quivering. It's its own being, its own entity. And when my legs push launch me, in one jump, from inside to outside my face bursts into the bloom of a smile that seems to have grown up from deep inside. Out here it's high, wide and wild and around me I can feel a growing, glistening green that's alive and pushing life into the most unlikely places, even up through cracks in the concrete.

I check that no neighbours can see me (they're not often out but you never know) and throw my hands in the air. But it's more than a 'throw'. It's really a reach, a stretching into the space of the sky. I want to see how far I can go, how much I can be part of this life-force, this blue and sunset-gold energy that reaches into my throat and demands a gasp of delight from me every time. At my feet, the seedlings are singing and even the weeds seem to be choosing to stay out of the beds, leaving my plants alone. They're heading in different directions, finding other water to suck up and other nutrients to gobble. Everything is more green, more alive, more shiny than yesterday.

I am going to visit my grandma. My heart is full. My hands are happy. The world is good.

I stay in the garden until the reds and pinks of sunset have muted into purple and grey and the plants themselves seem ready to rest for the night. I'm ready too. And the entry back into the house seems welcome. The garden has given me its gift of peace and I will take it inside, put it under my pillow and sleep with it.

Well, I would, if there wasn't so much homework to do. Maths, History, English. Even an assignment for Drama to hand in before the holidays.

I shovel down a TV dinner — Thai green curry and rice, courtesy of the corner supermarket and Mrs Billingham's Fresh Home Cooked Kitchen — and think (slightly wistfully) of Gabby eating freshly crumbed schnitzel with roast potatoes and her mum's Caesar salad. I saw her whipping the dressing as I left. She waved from the kitchen bench and all I could smell was herbs from the pots on her patio.

"Have you got homework?" says Mum, looking up from the couch where she's watching the news. It's her nightly routine; sit in front of the telly, surf the channels, complain that nothing's on and then read a magazine with something stupid playing in the background.

"Why don't you turn it off?" I asked once.

"It keeps me company," she said. She shrugged. "I don't know. It makes me feel less lonely."

"I'm here." I said it quietly. But I didn't make it a point. Even though it was true, I didn't want to sit all night with her on the cracked leather lounge, making conversation. Just the two of us staring at each other all night and thinking of things to say.

The TV stayed on.

Tonight I notice Mum's got her phone by her on the couch. She looks down at it every so often. Just checking. But quietly. Like she hopes I won't notice.

"Homework?" I say. "Um. A bit. There's a Science project coming up. I should probably think of some ideas of what to do."

I'm pretending not to watch her pretending not to watch her phone. She can't help herself. There's a small movement of the eyes, a sneaky walking of the fingers to touch the screen.

"Are you waiting for someone to call you?" I say.

She jumps slightly. Her chin goes up. Just a millimetre. But it's up.

"What?" she says, but I know what she's doing. That's my trick. Pretend you haven't heard the question so you can buy time and think of an answer.

"Phone," I say, gesturing with my head towards her handpiece, now transferred to her lap. "Someone calling?"

She shakes her head and throws both hands off her lap as if to prove she's got nothing to do with her phone. *Mine? No. I don't even know how it ended up here.* "No. No-one's calling. Why would you think that?"

I open my mouth but she's quicker. She's going on the offensive. *Attacking is better than defending.* It's something Gabby taught me. *Get people to notice you for the things you want to be noticed for. Turn up with socks on your head and they'll forget about your smelly feet.* I guess that's what Wally the Wombat was all about.

Obviously Mum's been talking to Gabby too. She puts her phone down on the other side, away from my eye line and looks right at me. "So. Homework. Science project. You going to do it? Do you need any help?"

"Yeah. No. I'm alright," I say. "I'll be in my room."

I turn away, out of the room and into the hallway, pulling the door behind me. It slams slightly. Just a little bang. It's not what I meant to do, but I keep walking anyway.

In my room my journal's on the desk. I flip it open to the next clear page, pull up a chair and grab a pen. I'm ready to write. About Grandma. About Gabby. About dreams and nightmares. Gardens and sunsets. But something is stopping me. It's a tiny, curly thought, nagging in the back of my head.

What is with Mum?

I make a quick decision. Instead of writing I draw. Quickly and firmly, pressing down on the blank page. It's a question mark. At first it's plain and large. Simple and clear. I sit back in my chair and look at it. And then I begin to add. Flourishes, dashes, dots. Flowers, even. And more question marks in different styles, shapes, sizes. First just a few, and then more and more. The white space fills up; the doodles are nearly falling off the page. The more I draw, the more I see to draw. The more there is inside my head, the more there is that wants to spread itself across the paper.

And then, it happens.

Over on the bedside table, the phone buzzes.

My hand freezes for a mini-second and a tiny shot of dread travels from my throat to my stomach. *Why am I worried?* The question passes through my head, almost unnoticed, but not quite. It's not like I don't want to talk to anyone who would text me, right?

Gabby. The twins. Liam.

Liam.

I let a small puff of air out of my mouth. I thought when you were going out with someone the nerves were supposed to disappear. Before he asked me out I was tingles and jingles and will-he/won't-he every second of the day. Now we're going out. But I'm nervous again. And I can't figure out why.

I push back the chair, get up and drag my feet across to the side of the bed. The mail notifications are all lit up. One new message. And yes. It's from him.

I hesitate for a second, and then I press the button. *Get*

it over with.

The message is long. I sit down on the bed to read it. And then, well, I don't really get up again. I let my back flop onto the doona cover and lie there with my knees still bent, feet still touching the floor. Liam's text plays through my head on repeat.

I love u so much but u don't seem to care. Don't u know guys have feelings too? We don't just turn off because it's not the right time or place. Yesterday at the park u pushed me away and this morning you didn't even tell me where u were. UR not being fair. If u like me, u have to prove it.

I read the last line again.

If u like me, u have to prove it.

And then again. And again. And again.

Prove it. Prove it. Prove it.

My heart is still beating. I like Liam. I like his eyes. His smile. His hair. His everything. I like him more than he realises. But what I don't like is that scared, out of my depth feeling I get when we're together these days. Maybe it's me. Maybe I'm wrong. Maybe I do need to *prove it*. I just don't know if I can.

chapter 7

While I'm asleep, I'm assaulted.

Well, nearly.

A greenish-black goblin balancing awkwardly on two back legs, is swinging a baseball bat at my head. But I'm not looking at the bat. All I can see is his blue eyes. Evil, blue eyes. I turn and run, panting, down the long, concrete corridors at school, desperately searching for somewhere to hide, someone to save me.

But there's nowhere.

And there's no-one.

At 2.41 am (that's what the green glow of the digital clock tells me) I wake up, skin sweaty and heart thumping and stumble to the bathroom. The tiled walls are cool against my hands. I lean my head on them, just for a different sensation. My eyes are open in the dark. They feel normal, like they could see anything I put in front of them, but I'm not fooled. I know if I turned the lights on they'd cower in fear. My body is prickly-alive, my chest breathing so quickly I feel like I might hyperventilate if I don't sit down.

But it's my mind that's really awake. My thoughts

are zooming like a roller coaster on continuous replay. Around, down, swirl underneath, pull up up up, smash to the bottom, and then around, down and everything all over again.

Liam, Grandma, how can I prove it? Why is Mum acting weird? Gabby eats croissants. Should I get a pet wombat? What do wombats eat anyway? Grass. Standing on the grass with Liam. Kissing. Drowning. Falling. Grandma.

I get back to my room and close the door. It probably wouldn't matter if I left it open. Mum's room is through the kitchen and down the hall. Practically at the other end of the house. But I don't want her to know that I'm up, awake, distracted, in the middle of the night.

I switch on the light. It jars my eyes but I blink through it until they adjust. I still have to keep them half-closed, my eyelashes protecting my pupils slightly. Everything I can see is slightly fuzzy. But I've got what I need.

My journal is still on the desk. I'm going to do something. I don't know if it will help, but it might. I'm going to draw every monster, every goblin, every giant that's ever attacked me in my dreams. Every wart and bump, drip of drool and piece of snot. I'm going to put them on paper, all there for anyone to see.

Go ahead. Chase me now. Try to kill me. I know what you look like. Someone's going to find you eventually, and then your fun will be over.

My pictures aren't great. I'm not an artist, but somehow, at nearly three in the morning, that doesn't seem to be important. All I care about is getting the images of evil, grinning, leering, dribbling monsters out of my head. I draw and draw until finally my yawns are too much to resist and I tumble back into bed and sleep. All night. Quietly.

Morning light makes things better. At 7 am, lying in the early sunshine, it's like the middle of the night panic was hardly real. A tiny, ridiculous, embarrassing episode that I'd make excuses for if anyone found out. "Oh, I was a little scared. You know how it is sometimes when you're a bit tired." *A little. A bit. A teensy smidge. Nothing, really, at all.*

My journal is closed on the desk. I must have shut the cover before I hit the pillow and I'm glad. Later, I might rip the pages out and burn them secretly behind the house. I check to see Mum's not around and swiftly put it in the top drawer. Secret. Quiet. Hidden. Not that I think she reads my journal. But you never know. I don't want her to freak out and for me to be answering odd questions this afternoon when I get home.

This afternoon.

The thought trips me up. I had arranged to go home with Liam after school. My heart takes a tiny extra skip and I bite my lip.

If I can just get through the next nine days until the holidays, I can go away to Grandma's and not have to worry about Liam. I just need some time. Then I can decide how I can *prove it* — that I like him like he likes me.

Keep it simple, I think. Stay with other people. Don't be alone. Tell him Mum needs me at home in the afternoon. *Fudge it until the holidays.*

If I can get to the end of term, I'll see Grandma. That

will make it all better.

My post-nightmare breakfast is toast and a fresh orange juice. Someone from Mum's work has an orchard full of orange trees and we've had so many recently that I've become the orange juice queen. I like it with the bits in it. They catch in my mouth but it's like I've got the whole orange. It tastes real. I don't know if juices are supposed to have any superpowers but they manage to clear my head after I've been screaming and running all night.

"Were you going out this afternoon?"

Mum's voice is loud in my ear. She sounds a bit frustrated. Like she's said it more than once.

"Sorry. What?" I say, looking up, brushing crumbs and monsters off the table.

"This afternoon. Did you say you were going out?"

"Oh. Um. Maybe not," I say. "Not sure." I sip my juice but it's more of a slurp as a bit of pith gets sucked up into my mouth.

"Weren't you going to Liam's?" she asks. She sounds surprised.

"Yeah. But I don't know," I say. I shrug. "I've got a lot of homework."

Mum looks like she's not sure what to do with that piece of information. Strictly speaking its true. All my teachers seem to have waited until the end of term to inflict us with essays and take-home tests. But I'm pretty well through most of them, except for the Science project which we have to start now and then continue after the holidays. Yeah, mostly done. And one afternoon at

Liam's wouldn't hurt me. But it's a good reason to give.

Mum looks at me. Her eyes are narrowed. It's one of her signs of worry. "Everything okay with you two?" she asks.

I fake a smile. "Yeah. Course."

"He's really nice, isn't he." She's still anxious. Checking for agreement on my face.

"Oh. I know." I nod enthusiastically but only my head is moving. "He's great."

"Okay." She steps towards the fridge awkwardly and gets an orange out. "These are good, right?"

"Mmm." I nod again. My shoulders join in this time. "Really nice."

The bus drives past the park with the plum blossom tree. Even just two days later more petals have fallen off the tree. The canopy above is thinner but the carpet underfoot looks like something you'd put in a little girl's pink and purple dream bedroom.

I get out my phone and read Liam's text again. I never replied to it. Now I think maybe I should have. If he brings it up I really don't know what I'm going to say. I want to tell him to be patient. To go slower. To be kinder. I want to ask him what was wrong with the way we were at the beginning. I want to know why we can't just go get ice cream. Sit together. Talk.

I close my eyes and imagine the conversation in my head. I say my piece and look at his face. Expectant. Waiting for the smile that melts me to my fingertips. Waiting for his eyes to sparkle at me again. There's a pause, in slow motion and then I see it. It's a smile that starts in the corners of his mouth and grows to cover his face. He opens his mouth and takes a breath. I think he's about to speak, to say, 'oh yeah, of course you're right Jazmine. I'm so sorry,' but no words come out. Instead he bends his head back, almost so he's looking at the sky and he laughs.

Cackles.

Guffaws.

Roars.

I disappear into the miserable nothingness of total and utter embarrassment. My eyelids slam open. I'm short of breath, shocked and jolted.

I don't think I'll be having that conversation.

Best to do what I do best: make an excuse, change the subject, avoid the issue.

When we pull up at school, I look out the window and see Liam, standing by the gate as normal, and suddenly all my fear disappears. He's so gorgeous with his tousled hair and his blue eyes that I can't think why I'm even worried about him. Maybe I'm just tired, I think. Maybe I'm a little bit intense. Maybe even a little crazy? *Just look at him*, I tell myself. *There's nothing to get upset about.*

The morning's dread drains away and instead a bubbling up of happiness takes its place. I push my way in behind all the other people in blue and white uniforms, jostling to get off the bus, and when I finally step off my smile is wide and relaxed. Liam steps forward to meet me, I step forward to greet him and we're just about to hug when there's a rush of air on my face and a noise in my left ear.

It's Olivia and Caitlin, and one look at their faces makes me think the school must have burned down. They've been running, as fast as they can, towards me and Liam and there's terror in their eyes.

"Jazmine!" they shout together. And then they're both talking at once, their words jostling for space. I can't understand them. It's too fast and I'm not keeping up. Liam sees my confusion and steps in.

"Stop!" he says. "One at a time. What's the matter?"

Olivia looks stunned; like she's been slapped on the cheek. She holds her face while Caitlin speaks up.

"It's Angela." She turns white as she says it. "She says you called her something terrible. She's says she won't stand for it. Jaz. She's going to fight you."

chapter 8

Caitlin and Olivia are the sort of people who get bouncy when they get upset. Their voices go high. Their words are quick. And their bodies move. Erin's a bit the same, but where the twins are scared, there's a streak of happy that shows up on Erin's face when someone else is in trouble. It's not obvious, but it's there in the slight curl of her lip, the brisk opening of her eyelids. If you have the eyes to see it.

I'm completely different. My body turns to a slow-moving, rubbery jelly. My stomach slips down to my knees and when I try to breathe and realise I'm slowly choking to death, I reach down inside me to find the air in my lungs has turned to water and is slowly leaking out. Instead of running, my feet send suckers and shoots into the ground. I'm planted in one place. When I try to speak my voice comes back to me, bouncing off glass walls. I'm in a slow-motion, silent snow globe of my very own and all the shaking in the world can't get me to move or respond.

"You. She wants to fight you."

Caitlin's looking into my eyes with a puzzled

expression. Olivia has a matching face and the two of them exchange glances that say *Doesn't she hear us? Doesn't she understand what this is?*

I blink. Peer at them. I feel like I'm out of my own body. Like the real me is somewhere, smaller, inside, looking out of my own eye holes like you'd sit at a window and admire the view.

Liam grabs my shoulder. "Jaz," he says. "You okay?"

I put my hands up to my eyes and just hold them there over my face. The pressure of fingers on my skin brings me back a little. I rub my eyes firmly, slide back into my body, open my eyes and ask a question.

"Me?"

Caitlin nods furiously. "I know, right?"

"I said you'd never call anyone, you know, a b...," says Olivia. She mouths the word, like it's too dangerous to say out loud. There's panic in her face. "But she says you did. You didn't, did you?"

Both girls are hanging on my answer, their big eyes wide with worry.

"No," I say. I shake my head slightly. "I didn't call her anything."

I can see the relief in the twins' faces. They let out identical gasps of air. "I knew it," says Olivia, turning to Caitlin. She has an 'I told you so' look on her face. "I knew she wouldn't have."

Caitlin shrugs her shoulders. "Well," she says, as a half aside to her sister. "I mean... maybe..."

Liam steps between us. "But Angela doesn't usually make stuff up," he says. "I mean, I know she's not the nicest person in the world, but I've known her since preschool. And I really don't think…" His voice trails off. "I don't get it. What's she trying to do?"

I know exactly what she's trying to do. She's still angry at me for the standing ovations I got in the play. But it wasn't as if I muscled in and pushed her out of it. She just can't stand to have anyone take over what she thinks is hers. And especially not to do a good job at it. She's taking a small, stupid, irritated conversation between herself and Gabby, twisting it so it looks way worse than it is, and then using the whole thing as an excuse to put me in my place.

Oh yes. I know exactly how this goes.

But even though I understand what's happening, I'm still terrified. My throat has gone to sleep and thinking straight is like finding my way through fog. I shake my head and move my mouth but nothing comes out.

"You should text Gabby," says Olivia. "Or I'll do it."

"Yeah," I say. There's cloud covering my head. "That would be… Can you?"

"I've got a phone," says Caitlin, urgently. She flips her pink leather cover open and presses out a message. Olivia's head comes in close to her twin. They're arguing about what they should write.

"I'll go talk to her for you," Liam says. He grabs my hand.

"Who?" I say. "Gabby?"

"No, silly," he says. "Angela, obviously. Come on. Let's go in. I'll sort this out for you."

I want to say no. *Just leave it. Don't make it a thing.* But he's already pulling me along and my legs are following dumbly. He parks me at our usual table and then walks across the quad to where Angela and her girls are sitting. I can feel the poison whiplash of their looks from here. The twins are in panic mode, buzzing around me and asking questions no one can possibly answer. *What's going to happen? Do you think she'll come over here?* I don't want to listen so I put my head in my hands and shut my eyes. A brown, warty, bristling gargoyle that spent all last Tuesday night chasing me with a live power line pokes its head into my brain and waves, leering, in the empty space in front of my eyeballs. No electric shocks this time. But still I gasp and snap my eyes open again.

Erin arrives and the twins rush over to update her. There's a lot of hand-waving, eyebrow raising and nodding and I can see Erin look over at me and then at Angela's group with a face that can't quite hide her excitement.

"For real?" She comes up to me and talks right in my face. "You going to do it?"

I look, frustrated, at her. "Do what?"

"Fight," she says. Like I'm the thickest person on the planet. "Are you going to hit her?"

I hold my hands palms up and shake my head quickly like I don't understand what she's even talking about.

"Um. No? I didn't even call her anything."

"Yeah, but she's saying you did. If you don't do anything now, it's like she's won."

"It's not even anything," I say. "You can't win if it's nothing."

Erin raises her eyebrows and steps back. "This is junior high school," she says. "You win. Or you lose."

I shrug and turn away. Liam's still over there with Angela and her group. She looks like she's angry, sulking on one side. One of her clone friends is up close to Liam, talking in his face. Lots of gestures. Nothing happy. I try to concentrate, to see what's going on but I'm tired. I can hardly keep my eyes open. All they want to do is shut but I can't let them. I'm too scared of what I'll see if I let them close. In front of me are the twins and Erin, alert and focused on the crisis. I turn my head further away looking for some rest for my brain, towards the direction of the gate.

There's no rest, but suddenly, and it's like there are trumpets playing, brassy and loud, in my head, there's something better than rest.

Relief.

Relief in the form of Gabby. No socks and no wombats. Just Gabby herself. And she's walking like she's got something to say. I put out my hand in a half wave as she comes closer. The fog around my muscles seems to lift and I tense a little, ready to stand up and tell her what's happened.

But she doesn't see me.

She walks right past me.

Right up to the table where Liam's talking to Britney.

Right up to Angela.

And then, the world slows down and it's like I'm looking through a pinhole lens because everything else is dark except for the light around Gabby and all I can see is her dropping her bag in one motion, stepping back on one leg and then forward on the other, all the while stretching out one arm in front of her and slapping Angela on the face.

Crack.

I'm sure I can't actually physically hear the noise of the slap but there's an electric shock imprinted on my brain followed by a sudden, total silence. Eight hundred heads — all the heads in the whole school — turn together to see Angela, stunned and breathless, holding her cheek in both hands and blinking, unbelieving, at Gabby who just stands in front of her, chest heaving and her hand slightly twitching beside her.

And then the noise erupts. Yelling. Whistling. Jeering. *Fight, fight, fight!* I can't see anything any more because Gabby and Angela are rushed at, the centre of a screaming, greedy swarm wanting more. The twins gasp and Erin grins and then they run towards the crowd as well, but I'm frozen in my seat, hardly breathing, replaying what I've just seen, over and over.

Weight back, foot forward, arm out, hand connect with face. Slap. And Angela, silent and shocked, but with her anger building.

The tension is rising. The whole school, except for me, who can't move, is yelling and shouting, closing in, trying to see two girls do violence to each other, until finally the teachers arrive.

Mr Singh, the Tech teacher and Miss Walker, the Deputy are screaming over the crowd. "Get back. Stop that." They're elbowing through, trying to reach Gabby and Angela. Another teacher, one I don't know so well, is taking mobile phones off the closer students. No one gets to post footage of a fight — the school makes sure of that. Finally, dusty and shaking themselves off, Gabby and Angela emerge out of the mess, a teacher holding each of them. I stand up now and make a move towards Gabby. "Are you okay?" I want to say, but too quickly she's marched off to the office block with Miss Walker, followed by Angela with Mr Singh.

I try to step after them but the streams of kids jostling back towards their areas are too strong to navigate through. I stop, my chest cold. It's pointless trying to chase after her anyway. I know what happens now. I've been through it all myself. They separate you, put you in a hard vinyl chair in a corner of the administration office and make you wait for your mum. Then they take you in to see the principal who talks while you listen. Or pretend to listen. If you're lucky, you go back to class. If you're not, you leave for the day. Or the week. Depending.

Weight back, foot forward, arm out, hand connect with face. Slap.

Yeah. Depending.

Liam, the twins and Erin are still talking, half to each other, but a little bit to Angela's friends who are now crying, their perfect hands clasped over their perfect faces. Every so often they wipe their noses and dab at their mascara and give their perfectly straight hair a flick. Liam's best friend, Dan, has joined them.

I look down for my bag and catch a glimpse of my hand. It's only then that I realise I'm shaking. And I can't stop. I'm like a patient with that shaking disease. The one that old people get. Parkinsons. There's a tear welling up in my eye as well. I imagine it sliding, zigzagging, down my shaking cheek followed by a million more, making up a crazy, jagged waterfall, and I know I can't stay here. I can't talk. Literally. My twitching mouth won't move to form words. And even if I could, I wouldn't want to talk. Especially not to the twins and Erin, all urgent and scandal-shocked, buzzing around in crisis mode. Not even to Liam. Gabby's gone nuts and I don't know when she'll be back, monsters are invading my dreams and all I have to do is make it to the holidays without getting into a fight. Any kind of fight.

I pick up my bag and walk. Strongly, quickly, curtly. I walk right away from there. Past giggling groups of year 7 girls, past the good looking Year 10 boys playing football, past the group of boys with their messy-haired leader from my Science class, gazing at me like rabbits in headlights. I walk right through the school. Straight to the bathroom.

chapter 9

It's easy to be invisible when no-one knows you're there. It's a lot harder to hide when people are looking for you.

When I get to the bathrooms there's a crowd of year 10 girls in the area near the sinks. They look at me curiously, like there's something they can't quite put their finger on, like there's something they should know. I can't tell what my face is saying. Sometimes when you try too hard to look innocent you end up looking guiltier than if you're actually to blame. I'm trying to look like anyone else, a normal person, not the girl who started the fight.

Not that I started it. But I've seen how things go. You can't escape the gossip and the rumours. They fly around like leaves in a storm, whipped up and frantic. If you fight back the wind stings your eyes and makes you cry. If you don't fight you end up cowering in the weather, soggy from the rain and covered in dirt.

The year 10 girls have figured out who I am. I can see an 'a-ha' moment spread over one face and then another, and then they are raising eyebrows at each other, making faces and sending looks. I feel my face prickle with embarrassment and make my escape into a stall, sliding the lock over with my still-shaking fingers. I collapse against the wall, half-shuddering, trying to keep my breathing quiet. My chest wants to sob, my eyes want to stream and my voice wants to scream. My hand moves, almost by itself, to cover my mouth, and I sink to a squat on the floor so I can squash the uprising in my stomach.

I want to shake Gabby. What was she doing? Did she really think slapping Angela in front of everyone was going to help? Standing up to a bully is one thing. I should know. I've done it. But I didn't do it in the middle of the quad. And I certainly didn't attack first. My thoughts are as shaky as my body. Gabby must have been trying to protect me but surely she's not stupid enough to think it would help. Or maybe it will. Maybe I'm wrong in always being the cautious one, the one who doesn't want to make a fuss, the one who gets through life trying to be safe.

I'm still breathing hard but the shaking is getting quieter until it's more of a tremor. I look at my hand and concentrate on making it still. I can do it, but only if I hold it against my knee. If I'm pressed in to something I can focus.

I haven't heard the bell, but that doesn't mean it hasn't gone. The Year 10s have gone and I'm alone, cold amongst the tiles and stainless steel. I pull out my phone and check the time. Ten minutes into class. Do I turn up late and make up an excuse that the teacher will believe or do I stay here and skip first period? And what about

Gabby?

I'll text her.

Gab. U okay? Are you suspended? What were you thinking?

The 'ting' of my phone goes when I press 'Send' and I wait, hopeful, for a reply.

There's nothing.

Three minutes go by and I send a different message.

Gabby? What's going on?

Ting.

Nothing.

Gab?

Ting.

I put my phone away. Maybe they've changed the rules. When I was nearly suspended, I could have used my phone. If I'd wanted. But back then I wouldn't have had anyone to message. They might be taking phones off people now. Or maybe Gabby's already in with the principal, Mr Fellowes. I can't imagine her sitting like me, head down, clinging to the sides of her chair. She'd be commenting on the room decor, asking him questions and trying to convince him to let her sew buttons all over her uniform blazer. *Just for fun, sir. We need more fun, don't you agree?*

I decide it's too late for class. I'll have to stay here for another 25 minutes. I shift so I'm more comfortable, without quite sitting on the floor, because it is a school bathroom, after all, but my comfort doesn't last long.

There's a crash outside. A door slams and then I hear my name.

"Jaz?"

"Jazmine? Are you…"

"…in here?"

It's the twins. I catch a breath and stand up quickly. On shaky-again legs. I'm not sure whether I should open the door and show myself. I'm half frozen, caught in between yes and no.

It's too late to hide though. They've heard me.

"I think she's…"

"Did I just hear…?"

And together, "Oh. In there!"

There's a knock on the door of my toilet stall.

"Jaz, is that you?"

I can't not answer, but my mouth can hardly move. I make an awkward sound, somewhere between 'yeah' and 'erm' but it's enough for them.

"Oh my goodness, we can't believe it. We've been looking everywhere…"

"…for you. Like, in every single girls' bathroom." Their voices are high and excited.

"Are you okay?"

"Are you coming out?"

There's no option. I turn the lock and the door swings open from under my hands. I'm left standing awkwardly in the stall, looking out.

"Oh Jaz!" Olivia's face crumples up and breaks into tears when she sees me. Caitlin, on twin remote control, does the same thing. The three of us stand together under the fluorescent lights, them crying and me patting them on the shoulder, trying to be comforting. I dig in my bag for a tissue packet (Mum insists I always have a spare).

There's a manky looking one under my lunch box so I pull it out and hand it to Olivia. She takes it gratefully, gives one to Caitlin and then delicately blows her nose.

"So, you saw what happened, right?" she says.

I nod. Glum. Who didn't see what happened? Who in this school doesn't know every tiny detail about Gabby slapping Angela?

"So apparently it was Gabby who was rude to Angela in class," says Caitlin, mopping at her eyes. "Angela's friends told Liam that Gabby called her a you know what." She looks apologetic.

Olivia carries on. "And then Gabby threatened her and told her she'd come and get her one day after school."

I shake my head. "That's so not what happened," I say. "They're making most of that up."

"But did you know Angela went for Gabby after she got slapped," says Caitlin. "She just grabbed her arm and pulled her down on the ground."

"Yeah, and she kicked her too," says Olivia. I shrug. Once the group gathered around them I couldn't see anything. And judging from this other story going around, it wouldn't be wise to believe everything. I can't be sure what's true or not.

"Did Gabby do anything else?" I ask.

"Don't know," says Caitlin. "But I know she's getting suspended."

"Like, for a week," says Olivia. Her eyes are as round as I've ever seen them. "Everyone's saying so. I mean, it's like Liam says, you can't just come and slap people out of the blue."

"I know," says Caitlin. "I mean, sorry, because Gab's your best friend and all that, but really, I think what she did was, like, totally, not cool. Everybody says so."

Olivia's face gets super-serious for a second. She comes in close to me. "Plus, everyone thinks that you should have been the one to sort it out, not Gabby."

I step back. "What?"

"Yeah," says Caitlin. She half shakes her head. "That's what everyone thinks. If you'd gone and just even talked to Angela, none of this would have happened. I mean, she might actually even end up with a black eye."

My mouth is open. A tremor has started in my top lip. I bite on it to stop it twitching.

"So people are blaming me because Angela might have a black eye?" I say.

The twins nod.

"And Liam thinks that what Gabby did wasn't cool?"

They nod again.

I shake my head, look around the room and go to speak, but no words come. My neck is twitchy and my arms are jerky. I can't stop moving my hands.

"That's it," I say. I shrug again. Ferocious. "I can't do this today. I can't do any of this." I grab my remaining tissues out of Olivia's hand. She gasps and looks shocked. I swing my bag over my shoulder and walk to the door. "Tell the teacher I'm sick and I had to go home," I say, looking back at the twins who now have eyes like tennis balls.

"Don't you have to get a sick pass?" stammers out Olivia, who always knows all the rules.

"Not today," I say. "Not today."

I turn and stride down the path. Behind me there's a small bleating of voices, but I'm done. Tomorrow I'll come back and deal with this. Today I've had enough.

There's a tiny catch in my heart as I walk out the school gates. *No pass. No permission. Jazmine, what are you doing?* I push it back down again and keep going, but not in the direction of home.

I need something. Something sweet. Something familiar. And there's an ice cream shop down the road. I've been there with Liam before. I ordered vanilla and he tried to make me like chocolate. Today I'm done with being told what I should and shouldn't do. Today I'm having vanilla because I like vanilla and I want to have vanilla.

The shop woman looks vaguely surprised when I storm through the doors, order a vanilla ice cream, *double scoop please,* in a waffle cone and slam my money down on the counter.

"Um, okay?" she says. "Do you want any toppings with that?"

I'm taken aback by the question for a second and then I think, *yes. Yes, I do want a topping. Not because anyone else says I want a topping, but because I will choose my own topping.*

"What kinds do you have?" I ask.

"Raspberry, Cherry, Caramel and Chocolate," she says. "Oh, also Ice Magic."

"Not chocolate," I say. "Or Ice Magic. I'll have raspberry."

She shakes the raspberry topping out of a glass bottle and nestles my ice cream in its little holder, standing upright with a napkin wrapped around it. Protecting it.

It doesn't need protection, I think, and I take the napkin off, deliberately wiping my fingers.

"I'll be outside," I say, to no-one in particular, because the shop woman has moved out of view.

I sit on one of the picnic tables out the back in the grassy area reserved for customers. It's the same picnic table I sat on with Liam. It's the same sky I sat under with him. The same grass I walked on. And yet everything is so different.

Then, my new life was just that—new. Tingly. Full of hope. I'd never had a door open for me in my life, and in a matter of weeks, everything changed. I had hundreds of doors to walk through. School, second chances, Mum, drama, feelings, friends. Love.

Now, it's not new any more. It's just… life.

When I was smaller I thought that at some point in my life I'd reach the place where everything had finally worked out. Where the happiness became permanent. I guess I thought of it like climbing a mountain. You hike and hike and it's hard, but you're always aiming for the top. Finally you get there and you're walking on air. You look at the view and it's amazing. All the effort you spent getting there is forgotten. You've made it.

No one ever said that you'd have to hike back down the mountain as well.

I kick my feet against the picnic table bench and screw up my face. The sun is warm on my arms and there are drips forming on my ice cream. I swirl my tongue right around the outside, cleaning it up.

"Vanilla is good," I say to myself. "And it will all be okay." I close my eyes, take a deep breath in. Then I let it out and open my eyes.

Through the sliding glass door into the shop I can see two people. One of them is a man with a beard. The other one looks just like my mum.

chapter 10

I slip off the picnic table so fast I'm like a lizard darting off the pavement. Before I even realise it, I'm squatting behind the table, trying not to be seen. My heart is beating so hard I can practically hear it in my head. Three facts pop into my head and start a chaotic dance.

Me not at school.

Ice cream.

Mum.

Is it actually her?

Yes. It totally is.

My brain is so busy trying to process the fact that I'm in the wrong place and things could get ugly that I totally forget to look at the person she's with. 'Tall' and 'beard' flash in quickly, kind of like when you drive through a new town and see a whole row of new signs. Interesting at the time but they're gone as soon as you turn the corner.

I can't look. I've got to work out what's going on here.

A) I can't let Mum see me.

B) Because I'll get in trouble.

C) And anyway, she wouldn't get why I've walked

out of school.

D) The only way out of this grass area is back through the shop.

E) Therefore I have to wait until she goes.

F) And seriously hope she doesn't come out here. Because, like, there is nowhere to hide.

I have two options, and two only, that I can see. I whisper them to myself.

Wait. And hope.

Oh, and then get the heck out of here.

Three options.

There's a drip of vanilla ice cream on my thumb and then another one on my finger. Crouching down behind the table, my ice cream has been in the sun and on a slight angle. I reach my mouth down to slurp up the drops but as I bring it back up I bang my forehead.

Hard.

Ow.

I feel like crying. This is the stupidest day ever. And now I'm getting sticky and sore trying to hide from my mother in an ice cream shop that I shouldn't really be in. A tear escapes out of an eye but I'm holding my ice cream in one hand and need my other one for balance so I can't wipe it. It slides down my cheek quicker than I would expect and drops off my face onto my shirt. I blink my eyes tight to try to stop another one that is beginning to bubble but there are too many and when I open them again everything is wet-fuzzy over my eyes so I can't see anything anyway.

Mum and whoever-it-is (probably one of the people

from work) are still in there. Taking their time. I'm not surprised. She takes forever to decide when we go out for anything to eat.

My ice cream is dripping again. I look down and see there's not too much left. Probably about a mouthful? I stuff the whole thing into my mouth and do that loose jaw kind of chewing where you're trying to manoeuvre it around without letting it spill out of your lips. Also, in the case of ice cream, without it hurting your teeth.

I don't succeed.

The cold hits my sensitive tooth at the back and I nearly let out a yell. I have to keep chewing and swallowing though because otherwise I'll drop the whole thing out of my mouth onto the grass and the woman in the shop will know exactly who the disgustingly gross customer was who spewed on her grass, and will maybe never let me come back. I manage to swallow it all down after a few gulps but I take some air down with it and then my throat and chest are super-uncomfortable for about a minute while it all settles down. Just when I think my ice cream traumas are over and my tooth has stopped hurting as well, I let out a large, loud, uncomfortable burp from all the air that went down.

I freeze, terrified. *Please don't let them hear me.*

After a couple of minutes I poke my head up. Gently. Gingerly. Just enough to see into the glass doors. The shop looks empty. I pick up my bag, sneak up to the entrance and stick my head around. I can see the woman who served me but there's no one browsing.

I lean back a little to see if I can get a glimpse of anyone through the front entrance but it seems clear. I let out a breath. It might be okay. I slip into the shop and walk through so I'm close to the door but not outside. I incline my head to get the best view possible.

No one.

I stick my head out of the door and look back towards the direction of school, which is clear, and then in the other direction.

My heart jumps, my stomach drops and I suck in another breath. It's Mum. And Tall Beard guy. They're holding coffees in a cardboard tray, walking away.

Not looking at me.

I decide to go the other way, back to school. I put a foot out of the shop, launch myself off and run, full tilt, away from my mother. My bag wobbles and skips on my back but I ignore it until I reach the first corner. After I turn, I collapse on the grass next to the path, breathing heavily. I've never really been a runner and honestly, I don't think I'm about to start.

But the breathing clears my head a little. I lean back and look up above me. The sky is as blue as I've ever seen it. Someone's planted peach trees along this street and the pink blossoms look like fairy popcorn pieces. But instead of it making me happy, I feel annoyed. The whole day seems so unfair. I don't think you should be allowed to have bad days under these sorts of skies. In the movies it goes cloudy and grey when things are bad. No one suffers when the sun is out. Why should I have to?

My fingers touch the soil under the grass. I wiggle them down and dig further in. I can feel dirt making its way into the spaces under my fingernails. It's familiar and comforting, and there's a shift in my head. It always happens. When I'm outside I see more clearly, breathe more deeply. And I realise that sitting here under a sky that's crazy-blue makes me smile.

I'll go back, I say. Almost out loud, but not quite. *I'll go back and see what's happened.*

Back in the quad, everything has changed.

And I mean everything.

The recess bell has rung and I walk back through the gates, up the path to see something I never expected. There are Angela and her friends, standing, chatting to the twins, Erin and Liam. At our table. Together. And they don't look like they're about to punch each other.

What is this?

I slow down my steps and look more closely.

Britney and Erin are talking to each other, leaning against the table. The twins are giggling with another of Angela's friends. Phoebe, I think her name is. Gabby's nowhere to be seen. Angela's cheek is reddish and there's a bruise on her arm but apart from that she looks fine. Happy, even. She's sitting next to Liam, her head resting, tilted, on her hand, facing him. She shakes her hair out so it falls over her arm, gently brushing the table top.

Is she... *flirting?*

My whole body heaves with a shudder that begins at my toes and continues to my eyelids. Do other people's worlds turn upside down this quickly? Can your enemies turn into friends and your friends turn into enemies in the space of 35 minutes? In the time it takes you to eat one vanilla ice cream and walk back to school?

My feet feel twitchy. They want to move. I could turn now and run out the gate again and no one would have seen me. I glance around behind me. It's an option. I pull my mouth to one side and consider it, but then I bring myself back.

Gabby would say to be brave, I tell myself, although my stomach is caught up in my ribs somehow.

I walk up to the group, put my bag down and go to sit at the table. There's a lull in the general noise levels.

"Jaz," says Olivia, breaking the silence. "We thought…"

"We thought you'd gone," says Caitlin. "Like, home."

I shrug.

"I felt better," I say. "Plus it's a long walk." I turn to look at them directly. "Did you have Science? Did Mr Cox say anything about the projects?"

There's a half second where it looks like Caitlin, whose mouth is still gaping open, is reorganizing her brain.

"Yeah. Um. So he said we've got to find our own groups and pick our topics," she says. "Before the holidays. Then when we get back we can get straight into it."

"Cool," I say. I turn to Liam and Angela who haven't taken their eyes off me. "Hey."

Angela makes a face, rolls her eyes slightly and tosses her hair. She looks away. Liam looks like he still doesn't know what I'm doing there.

"Hey," he says. He manages a half smile. "They said you went home. I was going to call you and see if you're okay."

"You don't need to," I say. I shake my head, just slightly and smile. "I went for a bit, but then I thought I'd come back. Too much explaining to Mum."

"Totally." He nods in agreement. Then he signs in Auslan, *You okay?*

I shrug. *I guess,* I sign back. *What happened to G?*

Suspended. He mouths the word at me. He probably doesn't know the sign for it. Then he holds up a finger. *One week.*

My chest loses air and I slump a little. I signal with my head to Liam. *Come with me.* I need to talk to him without Angela there. He looks over to where I'm pointing to and makes a little face like, *okay.* Then he gets up, really casual and heads over to the Science building. I grab my bag and follow.

When we get around the corner, out of sight of Angela, Liam grabs me around the waist.

"I was so worried about you," he says, almost in my ear. "Are you okay?"

"I'm fine," I say. I sort of disentangle him from me and try to take a step back. "I just need to know what happened. And why are they all at our table now?"

"Gabby just kind of went off," says Liam. "I was over there, you know, trying to talk to Angela about it all, like I said I would, and then Gabby just came right up and slapped her in the face. It was the loudest thing I ever heard." He shook his head. "Crazy. That girl's off her rocker. She's nuts."

I look at him like I can't believe what I'm hearing, but

he's talking again.

"I mean, anyway, it turns out Angela wasn't going to fight you. She hardly knew what I was talking about."

"Is that what she said?" I ask. I'm suspicious.

"Yeah, totally," he says. "And I believe her. I really do. It was probably one of the guys she hangs out with who made it up and spread it around."

"When did she say it?" I ask.

"She just told me now," he says. "At recess. She couldn't before. She was in with the deputy and crazy Gabby, sorting it all out."

"So it's a whole week?" I ask.

"Yeah," he says. "And Gab deserves it too. I mean, she's nuts going after someone like Angela. She can't win."

I take another step back. This conversation is confusing. This morning Angela was the evil villain of the quad. Now it's turned into being totally Gabby's fault.

"But Gab was standing up for me," I say.

"Well, she shouldn't have," says Liam. "Angela was being totally fine about everything, plus I was looking after it, and then Gabby just came in and attacked her." He steps back in closer to me. "Anyway, as long as you're okay…"

His hands come back to my waist and he's pulling me in for a hug and I can see that he wants to kiss, but my head is spinning and my world has gone cuckoo and all I want to do is sit and think.

"We can't," I say, turning my head away. "We're at

school. This is not the right time."

He steps away and pulls his hands back. His face is dark and his eyes look sharp.

"It's never the right time for you, Jaz. Come on. I wasn't asking for much. It's just a kiss."

My heart sinks and I feel a burning guilt and a terrible ugliness that spreads its sticky fingers all over my lungs.

"No, it's just..." I begin, but he's still mad. "Sorry," I say. "I'm really sorry." I take a breath and force out some words. "I just got upset. I didn't know what I was saying."

I step closer to him, touch his shoulder and offer him my face but my heart isn't in it. "You can, if you like."

He circles around, grabs my waist and kisses me. It's not gentle. When he stops I have to wipe around my mouth.

"I'll see you at lunch," he says and walks off.

chapter 11

The next three days are a blur. I go to school and sit with my old friends and my apparent 'new' friends, Angela and her crowd. They mix, talk and crack jokes like they've been hanging out for years. I avoid Angela as much as possible but I smile at Liam, sit next to him and act like I'm okay, except when he wants me to come with him behind the Science building and then I have to make excuses about needing to go to the bathroom.

I check my phone practically every ten minutes.

Still no replies from Gab.

I've texted her, left messages, tried to call and generally been a cyber-stalker.

Nothing.

"Maybe they went away," says Mum, when I tell her Gabby's not at school (but not the reason why). "Or maybe she's sick and forgotten to charge her phone." She shrugs. "It's probably nothing bad."

She's right, of course. I mean, it could be that she feels stupid or embarrassed or guilty. But that's not really like her. What would be more normal is for her to be over here, bouncing on my bed, telling me exactly how it feels to slap Angela.

Which I'm sure would be basically this: "Awesome!"

There's nothing to do but wait. She's sent me approximately 72 texts a week every week since we became friends last term. She'll be back.

She's not back at school, though. I guess I didn't really expect that she'd get off her suspension before the end of term, but after what happened to me, with Miss Frazer, I thought maybe there might be some special deal she could do.

Apparently not.

She stays suspended and away. But the word obviously hasn't gotten out to all the teachers. On Friday in Science, Mr Cox takes the roll.

"Where's Gabby? This is the second lesson she's missed," he says.

I put my head down. Someone else will tell him, surely? But for once, the class stays silent.

"Jazmine? You'd know where she is, yes?" he asks.

I take a deep breath and look up, only at him, avoiding everyone else's eyes.

"She's suspended, sir," I say.

"Oh," he says, obviously surprised. "Why?"

I look back down at my desk. "Fight," I say, softly. It's kind of a mumble. He lifts his eyebrows and glances back down at his list.

"Hmm," he says. It's the sort of noise you make when you'd actually rather say a whole lot of other stuff but you can't.

"Okay," he says. "Well. We'll move on. I'm guessing

that you all still need some time to find your groups and choose your topics for next term's project. You've got ten minutes now. Sort yourselves out. Groups of four. Go."

He looks at his watch and stands back while everyone gets out of their seats. There's a buzz of 'will you?' and 'what do you think?' and then some giggles and hand slapping.

I don't move.

This is the stuff I hate. This is what makes me feel like melting, red-faced, hot and bothered into my plastic seat. Teachers think they're doing kids a favour when they let us 'sort ourselves out' but it's just another battle you've got to fight. I know, without looking around, that Caitlin and Olivia will have buddied up with Britney and her best friend Stella. The four of them haven't stopped giggling in three days. Liam is in a higher Science class so he's not here. And Gabby's obviously not in her normal spot next to me. I have no options.

I'm sitting, quietly, dying inside, when there's a tap on my shoulder. I almost jump and then I'm so embarrassed about being startled that I can feel a red blush rising fast.

"Jazmine."

It's the messy haired kid from across the quad. The one with the science nerd type friends. Alvin. He's standing beside me with his hand reaching out to my shoulder. When he sees me look at it, he pulls it back so suddenly that I think he's spring loaded.

"Oh, sorry," he says.

"It's okay," I say. And then I don't know what else to say so I just look at him.

"Um, we need a fourth person," he says. "I mean, we don't just want you to be the *fourth* person. You're not just an afterthought. I mean, we'd like you to be in our group anyway. You're not with anyone are you? I mean, not, like, 'with' anyone. I'm just asking if you're already in a group." He stops, clearly confused.

He's so clumsy that I feel I can smile. I follow his gesture to the back of the room where two other boys are clustered around the lab desk. They grin and wave at me. I'm so surprised that I actually wave back.

"Um, okay?" I say. I look back over my shoulder, just to see that I'm right about the twins and Britney. Yes. They're giggling over in the corner. I shake my head slightly, like I'm trying to clear it, and then smile, a little bit brightly at Alvin.

"Yeah, sure," I say. I grab my books and move to the back.

Alvin smiles sideways, awkwardly, at me. I grin back. *If only Gabby could see me, hanging with the science geeks.* As they scuffle and shuffle to make room at the table, I pull out my phone and check my messages, just in case she's come back to life since I last looked, fifteen minutes ago at lunch.

But there's still nothing.

It's confusing. This is not Gabby. It's *so* not. This makes me want to bang on her front door and stick my head in and yell, "Where are you?" but I haven't even been able to do that. On Wednesday afternoon Mum took me shopping to get a new swimsuit for when I go to Grandma's. On Thursday she made me stay home and finish my final English essay for the term. Today is the only time I could go before the holidays start, but I know Mum is panicking about me going away, and plus I'll have to pack.

I bring myself back to the lab desk. Alvin and his two friends are discussing options for the project.

"I've been researching things we can do," says one. He's a little guy with short brown hair and a high voice. "There's one experiment where you can test how much bacteria grows in your spit. And then you can compare it to dog spit."

I screw up my face. "Eww," I say. But Little Dude looks at me in surprise.

"That's the coolest thing ever," he says. "And I've got a dog that drools heaps so we'll have plenty of dog spit to use."

All three guys start to talk at once. Their faces are lit up like they've just won free movie tickets to something based on a comic strip.

"Um," I begin. Tentative. Not wanting to make waves. "Do you think, maybe..." but they're not hearing me. I look around, waiting for someone to step in for me. Gabby usually comes to my rescue if she sees I'm not happy. Liam as well. But as soon as I think it, I catch myself. Liam's not here. Gabby's who-knows-where. Unless I want to spend the first five weeks of next term looking after test tubes of Fido saliva I'm going to have to say something.

I half stand, pushing my stool out behind me. It makes a scraping noise on the lino floor and the boys stop talking for a second.

"No," I say. It comes out more strongly than I aim for. "Sorry, but no. That's a totally gross idea and I can't do it."

Little Dude, and the other guy, who I only know as Cammo, look genuinely disappointed. Alvin's face is different. He looks apologetic.

"Oh, yeah, right," he says. He turns to the others. "You guys. We have to think of something else."

Little Dude scrambles through a bunch of papers stuffed in his notebook. "Electromagnetic fields. Done that. Eyesight charts. Boring. Basic machines. Didn't we do those in Year 6?"

"No," says Alvin. "We should ask Jazmine."

There's an electric second where, suddenly, six eyes are directed at me and me only. Six, science-loving eyes, looking at me, who'd prefer to be anywhere else, really, than here planning an experiment.

"Jazmine. What do you want to do?" Alvin asks, and I twist my mouth, not because I'm thinking but because I'm nervous. *What do I want to do?* Who would know? I pick up my pen and tap it on the table. *Tickita tickita tickita.* They're still focused on me, waiting for an answer. I'll have to say something; I just don't know what.

I scratch next to my nose. It makes me feel better. "Um, I like plants?" I say. And then I sit down, scrape in the stool and sit, hunching slightly, on my hands.

Cammo shrugs. "Plants are cool. We can do plant stuff." He turns to Little Dude. "Sebastian, what have you got?"

Sebastian digs through his sheaf of papers again. His

enthusiasm is back. "Yeah, I found this one. It's pretty cool. You can test leaves when they're green and find out what colour they're going to be in autumn."

There's a general murmuring of approval. Alvin puts out his hand. "Can I see? What do you have to do?" Sebastian gives him the sheet and Cammo sticks his head over Alvin's shoulder. There's some pointing and discussion and a few nods and grunts. Alvin hands the sheet to me.

"What do you think?"

I pause for a tiny second and then take the piece of paper from him. Confidently. Like I actually would know what I'm doing. Like I have an opinion about science projects. I read it quickly and then hand it back.

"That looks fine," I say. "Let's do that."

"Cool," says Alvin. And just like that, I am an official science geek.

I don't tell Liam.

After all, it's not as if I *have to*. It's not as if there's some kind of rule which says you should tell your boyfriend every single thing that happens in Science. It's just a group. For a project. Which I'm not really that interested in anyway.

But I still feel a teeny little bit bad. A little bit, I don't know, guilty.

He grabs my hand as we walk towards the gate where the buses line up. I hold it, free and happy because it's the holidays, but also because I want to make it up to him, make him feel better.

"I'm going to miss you Jaz," he says. "I was really

hoping we'd hang out heaps these holidays. This whole grandma thing seems really random."

"I know," I say, trying to keep a light-hearted tone. "I couldn't believe it when Mum organised it. I can't wait."

"And it's the whole two weeks?" His face looks deflated. I feel a little sorry for him.

"Yeah," I say. "But I'm not sure exactly when I'll be back on the last weekend. Maybe we can do something then."

"You're going to miss Angela's party," he says, and gives my hand a squeeze. I stiffen up. It's not conscious. It just happens.

"Angela's having a party?" I say.

"Yeah. We're all invited. Didn't she tell you?"

"Um, no," I say. I want to say more but I hold it in.

"On the middle weekend. It's going to be awesome." His face brightens up. "But you'll miss it."

"Is it her birthday?" I try to show some interest but he shrugs.

"Don't think so. It's a 'just because' party, she says."

"Just because?"

"Just because she wants to, I guess."

My face burns and my brain is starting a slow smoulder, but it's not for any reason I can figure out. Angela can have a party if she wants to. I guess I just don't want her to want to.

My bus turns up and I wait for the crowd to push on.

"Okay," I say. "Well, have a great holiday."

"How can you say that?" Liam says. "Without you."

"You'll be fine," I say. I hold his other hand. "I'll be

back super quickly." He steps in to give me a kiss and I instinctively dodge so it ends up being a peck on the cheek.

"No more?" he says. He has his puppy dog eyes on.

"After the holidays, okay?" I say. "I'm nervous about seeing my grandma again right now." I turn to go, but I don't want to leave him sad. "Bye?"

He turns and kicks his heels against the concrete. "See ya. Two weeks." Then he walks away and doesn't look back. I nearly miss my bus because I'm still staring after him, hoping he'll turn around and flash me a Liam smile to ease my stomach nerves.

"Getting on?" the bus driver growls finally, and I scurry up the steps as the doors hiss and clunk behind me.

Later, Mum makes me pack, but not before I force her to promise to take me over to Gabby's place later.

"Al-*right*," she says, finally. "O-*kay*. But only if you're done before seven. I don't want to drag myself out at night if I've got to get up that early in the morning to put you on the bus."

I'm done by 6.45, bag zipped and extra snacks for the two and a half hour trip stowed away in a lunchbox as well, and present myself to Mum.

"Can we go?"

"Fine," she says. "Let's get in the car. But I'm not staying long, okay? Fifteen minutes max."

It's a 12 minute drive to Gabby's place, across town and into the new housing estate. Mum listens to one of her 90s music evening shows on the radio while I alternately check my phone and stare out the window. I want to ask her about Ice-cream Beard Guy. He's been popping into my head on and off, just pressing tiny little question mark buttons in my brain, but I can't say anything because, obviously, I'm not supposed to have been there. But what would I say anyway? *Hey, Mum, do you always have company when you go to get the office coffees?*

"She probably just dropped her phone in the loo or something." Mum breaks into my head.

"What?" I say.

"There's probably a really good reason for her not calling," says Mum. "Or else she cracked the screen and had to put it in for repair. Like you'll have to do unless you buy yourself a proper phone cover."

I make a face at her.

"Well, it's just weird," I say. "Hey, it's the second on the left here."

Mum glances at me, annoyed. "I know. How many times have I brought you here?"

She pulls into Gabby's street and up to the house. It looks different. The blinds are all pulled down.

"That's funny," I say. "Her mum usually has them up."

Mum shrugs. "Maybe they're out," she says. "They could have gone away for the weekend."

I get out of the car. The house seems quieter for some reason, even without the blinds, but I can't pick why. I walk up the path and knock on the door. Twice.

No answer.

When I try to look through the crack between the edge of the window and the blinds, Mum yells at me from the car. "Jaz. That's rude."

I shrug. "I can't see anything anyway. Do you have any paper and a pen? I'll at least leave her a note. Then she'll have to call me, right? Maybe I'll give her Grandma's number too."

Mum digs around in her bag and produces a tiny scrap of old shopping list paper and a stub of a pencil. I write carefully, leaning against the glove box.

Gab. Where are you? You have to phone me. I've gone to my Grandma's for holidays. 88456243. Call me!!!!

I push the note through the letterbox and stand for a second, looking at the house. Then I screw up my mouth in frustration, breathe out sharply through my nose, turn on my heel and get back into the car.

"Home?" says Mum.

Home, I sign.

We're silent in the car and quiet through the front door at home. But for once, I *want* to talk. I want to say, all in one outpouring, that I can't wait, that I'm dying to see Grandma, that I can't believe this, this thing, of me on a bus, travelling, bounding into my grandma's arms after more than four whole years, is actually happening.

I want to say it, but Mum's happy (at least I think she is) and I don't want to wreck it. If I start on about Grandma, her face will go tight and she'll say things like "mmm, good," without actually meaning them.

I look across the kitchen at Mum. Her back is turned; she's making her evening cup of tea. I want to ask her

96

why. Why it happened, why we moved away without so much as a visit or a look back. Why hasn't Grandma been in touch for all these years?

Why can't the two women I love the most in life just sit down and talk to each other?

My head is full but my mouth is empty. "I'll head to bed," I say.

She swivels slightly. "Good idea."

And then it's time for all those little before bed rituals, the teeth, the glass of water, the kiss on the cheek goodnight. I hold my face next to Mum's for an extra second.

"Do you mind?" I say, in an almost whisper that I can't even hear.

Mum pulls back so she can see into my eyes. "What are you talking about?"

I turn my head a little so I'm half hiding from her gaze. "Do you mind that I'm going?" I say. "To see her. I mean... you know." But I still can't say what I want to say.

"She's your Grandma," Mum says. "And it's not your fight. It's between me and her, not you." She shrugs. "I hope you have a really good time." She turns to point to my bedroom. "But now? Get some rest."

I don't.

At two am I'm running away from more things that want to kill me. *Seriously? Again? If this wasn't so scary I'd be bored.* I'm tired beyond words and all I want to do is give up but they're getting closer, and I know that, as usual, if I don't run I'll be dead.

And then, in my dream, my brain clears; the fear and terror melt away and it's as though I've never understood the most obvious truth in the world.

"If I just ask the monsters to stop chasing me," I say, "we can all just live our lives."

It seems so simple. Why did I not think of this before?

"You've got your own things to do," I call, my words tumbling into the darkness. "Don't chase me anymore. I'm tired of it. I won't bother you if you won't bother me." I wait, straight-standing and expectant in my dream landscape, ready for some kind of sign.

But there's nothing.

"Hello?" I call again. "Are you there?"

I hear the tiniest rustle behind me. It's the sort of noise I could never hear if I was awake, but for some strange reason, I'm never deaf in my dreams. I look around quickly but there's nothing to see in the dark. My body turns to terror and I know there will be no agreement, no peaceful 'you go your way, I'll go mine'. There's no way out of it, this endless running, no matter which way I look.

I wake up crying.

chapter 12

The place where you catch the bus in our town is nothing like those crazy-busy bus terminals you see in movies. It's a too-small shelter on the side of a road with not even an office behind it. We're 15 minutes early and I'm worried it's the wrong place but then a car pulls up and an old man in shorts and long socks with a small black suitcase gets out of the passenger side. He adjusts his grip on his case, moves to the other side of the shelter and nods to us. Mum makes a quick face back at him, one of those grimace smiles that says, "Yes, we're in this together." She checks the time on her phone and then moves to the edge of the footpath to see if she can catch sight of the bus.

"I'll miss you," I say, when she comes back to sit next to me.

She glances over at my knees. "Me too. I mean, I won't miss myself." She smiles. "I'll miss you."

"What are you actually going to do while I'm gone?"

She shrugs. "Not much. Work, mostly. You know."

"Nothing different at all?" I ask.

"Maybe a few things," she says. "I might go out with

a friend."

I'm genuinely surprised. It's the first time I've ever heard those words from her lips.

I sign to her. *Who will you go out with?*

Work people, she signs back. *Just some people from work.*

"What are their names?" I ask. I want to know. She's never gone out with people from work before. I want to say, "Do they have beards?" but have to hold my tongue.

She shrugs again. "Just people." Checks her phone. "Only four minutes until the bus comes."

The work friends disappear into the background as a pinch of excitement grabs my stomach. It's followed by a burst of worry. I've never left Mum before. I mean, not ever, except to go to school. I even managed to get out of the overnight school excursions that started from about Year Four, mostly by 'forgetting' to take notes home until it was too late, but occasionally by coming down with an illness that lasted about as long as the excursion.

Now I'm leaving, by choice, for two whole weeks. I grab Mum's hand, tight. She looks startled.

"You'll be fine," she says. "You'll have fun."

"Maybe we should just go home," I say. I'm breathing heavily now. My stomach is a hard ball inside me. "Why is everything in life so scary?"

Mum looks at me and narrows her eyes. She reaches down between her feet and pulls her handbag up to her lap.

"I should probably give this to you," she says, unzipping the bag and bringing out a blue envelope. It looks old; worn and a little soft around the corners.

I take it in my hand and turn it over. Whatever's

inside feels firm, like cardboard.

Like a photograph.

I tip the flap and half pull what's inside into my hand, and there, staring, smiling up at me are four faces. Me, about six years old, in a yellow sundress and with my hair in pigtails. I have no front teeth and my smile looks even wider with the gaps. Mum is standing behind me in jeans and a white t shirt. Her hair is long and straight. And blonde. I'd forgotten how she used to dye it. Next to her is Dad, in his moustache phase. His arm is draped around Mum's shoulder and the two of them are tipping their heads toward each other with happiness. My eyes move to his other arm. It's tucked around another woman, wearing an orange and turquoise shift and a huge amber necklace. Her hair is short and red, to match her shoes.

It's Grandma.

And she's smiling right at me.

I gasp. "I remember this," I say, turning to Mum. "It was my birthday. We had a picnic in that park. And Grandma gave me a really funny present. Hiking boots. I just kind of looked at them and thought, 'what the heck?'"

Mum grins wryly. "I can't remember that. But it sounds about right." She looks at me. "Do you still want to come home?"

I sit up, pulled up straight, like the old man's socks.

I shake my head. "I'm going," I say. "I have to see Grandma again."

There's a rush of wind and a flurry of dust and the

coach pulls up. Mum stands up and pulls at my clothes. "You're just a bit scruffy," she says, adjusting the collar on my t-shirt. "There. Got everything?" She hands me my ticket and I swing the backpack on my shoulder.

"Okay, bye," I say and kiss her on the cheek and she kisses me back and holds me in a hug for an extra second. I pull away and go to step onto the bus but the old man is there before me and I don't want to be rude. A thought pops into my head and I have another mini-panic.

"Mum!" I say. "Can you water my garden? I forgot to ask."

She nods quickly.

"I mean it. The new plants will die if you don't. Especially if it's windy." I make the sign for *die*.

She nods again and signs, O*kay. I love you.*

You too, I sign back.

And then I step onto the bus and walk up the stairs and the doors close behind me with a clatter. For a moment I feel disoriented, like I'm nowhere and then I think, *Okay, just find a seat,* and I'm sitting down on blue patterned velour with maroon swirls. The bus pulls away and soon, outside the plastic, sound-proof window, streets and trees and houses are flashing by, and it's just me who's here, on my own, flying through the crazy world in a velour-coated capsule. My fingers realise they're holding something and when I look down to see what it is I remember the photo and Mum and Dad and Grandma's smiles and the hiking boots and I smile back.

It's not just me here, I think. *It's me. And my family.*

I'm supposed to put my bag in the overhead thingy but I've stuffed it down by my feet instead. It's easier to get what I need out of it. And right now I need something I haven't used for a few days.

It's my journal.

I skip past the drawings of monsters and scary ghouls-of-the-night. Better not to think about them when the sun is shining and the sky is blue. A new page, somewhere towards the middle of the book is where my fingers land. It's white and clean. Shiny, even. I hold the photograph of gap-toothed me and happy parents and non-fighting Grandma so that it's in the middle of the page, like I'm working out where to glue it in. And then I lean down again and scratch around in my bag for a pen.

Weird how you can go from writing words to drawing pictures to express how you feel. When I first got my journal I was all about writing letters to Dad and finding the right words to say. Now I'm sketching the things I need to think about; the things that mean something to me. It's different in some ways; the same in others.

I'm drawing Grandma; her short, cropped fringe; her twinkly but determined eyes; her flash of a smile. I need felt tips or pencils or *something* that will give her colour but even just with a black biro I can imagine her brightness. Even on the bus, with the aroma of plastic and long-distance passengers, I can smell her perfume.

The glare through the window is getting harsher. Outside the town has disappeared and all I can see is road and grey-green, scratchy bushland flashing past. I close my eyes to block out the speed but the light and shadows still flash across my face and I can feel every sway and jiggle of wheels on bumpy road. Across the aisle, the man with the long socks is reading the paper and behind me are two older ladies who look like friends. Maybe even sisters. When I get up to visit the tiny toilet at the back their heads are close and I can see them chatting over a magazine.

By the time I've eaten, read and drawn in my journal, the two and a half hours of the trip are nearly gone and before I'm ready signs begin to flash into view. Car dealerships, hardware barns and then the beginnings of cafés and barbecue chicken shops. To the left a green arrow points the way to a beach and a harbour.

The gnawing in my stomach is back with a vengeance. I look down at the drawing of Grandma on my page. I'm sure it looks nothing like her. She'll have changed, or I'll have changed. Will I even be able to recognise her? Am I doing a completely stupid thing, going to spend a whole fortnight with someone who hasn't wanted to speak to me or Mum in four years? Does she even want me now?

The driver makes an announcement across the loudspeaker. With the dull hum of the bus in my brain I can hardly understand a word but then the brakes come on and the bus slows down and it hits me.

This is it.

This is really it.

The engine goes into an idle and around me people are standing, stretching, searching for their stuff. The old man with the socks lifts his bag carefully down and nods politely to me. I smile back tentatively. People are filing off the bus slowly, all crowded together, elbows and knees jostling for space, but I haven't joined them yet. I'm huddled with my bag in my seat. I know, though, I have to get up. I have to get out. And when the line thins, I join the end and shuffle out into the daylight.

My eyes blink in the brightness. The coastal glare is something you never forget. Immediately I'm five again, getting out of the car at Grandma's place, blinking and blinded, but happy to be there.

And then I see her. As she is exactly the same as she was when I was five, smiling, half clapping her hands, bobbing up and down on her toes, waiting for me.

I stop. My feet are on concrete but my head is in the clouds. A smile spreads from one ear to the other and then I can't help myself. I throw my bag down and I run full tilt towards her, towards Grandma, towards the smell of plum blossoms and the promise of safety.

"Jazmine."

It's just one simple word but it sounds like flowers and excitement and adventure and I love you.

I have no words. All I can do is hug. She grabs me tight around the shoulders and hugs me back and it feels like home.

Chapter 13

Grandma's house is out of town, heading up a winding, bumpy road towards the escarpment. It's not where I remember.

"Did you move?" I ask.

"I sold it about four years ago," she says. Easily.

"Do you miss the old one?"

"Wait until we get there."

I wait. And then we turn a corner into a dirt driveway and immediately I understand. Grandma's new house has a view. And it's not just any view. From her verandah she can see for miles up and down the coast.

"It's amazing," I say and she smiles.

"You always loved the views from the lookouts when we used to go walking," she says. "When I saw this place I knew it was right. And it has a great garden."

My heart jumps.

"Can I see?"

She takes me around the back of the house. "It's mostly around here. I'm working on the front more now. I've put in all these cuttings from…" She turns to look at me. "Oh. Are you okay?"

I'm crying. That is to say, there are tears coming out of my eyes and slipping down my cheeks. But it's not from sadness. It's because finally I've seen what a garden should be, what it could be. Sweeping trees, extravagant roses and cheerful, bobbing flowers in beds. A vegetable patch with a blueberry bush.

And now I get it. I understand why my character, Mary Lennox, changed so much in the play of *The Secret Garden* we did last term.

I'm not crying because I'm unhappy. I'm crying because I'm delirious.

Grandma puts her arm around me and we stand together and take in the scent of the blossoms.

"Yours are still out," I say, wiping my eyes and pointing to a pink plum tree. "At home they've all fallen off."

"It's always a little later than most, that one," she says. "And speaking of later. I need a cup of tea."

The house is as small as our terrace at home but for some reason it feels bigger. It might be the way Grandma's furnished it, with new, simple furniture and big colours. Or it might just be the light that pours in from the glass doors. Our house is old and dark. Sometimes Mum describes it as cozy, but maybe it's actually just poky.

There's another difference. In this house there are no piles of paper, no knick-knacks, no bits and pieces. Not like our cluttery cupboards. Also, there are no pictures in frames. But there's no time to think about that because Grandma is showing me to my room.

"You're down here," she says, leading me down the

hall. There's a big bed with a grey satin cover on it, but my eyes hardly see it. They're too busy being dazzled by the pile of orange and pink and red cushions spread all over it.

"Why don't you put your stuff away and get comfy," she says. "You can come out when you're done."

She closes the door behind her and I sit on the bed, my bag on my knees. The mattress feels softer than mine at home. The room is bigger. Even the air tastes different. I never realised that travel could make even breathing into a new experience.

A chest of drawers stands against the wall on the other side of the room. On it is a dish of large, coloured beads, a small mirror and two little red birds. Paper maché, I think.

Above it is a framed print, all blue and white, with a boat at the top and words underneath. It says: 'A ship in a harbour is safe. But that is not what ships are built for.' I raise my eyebrows and shrug. *Okaaay.*

There's a view through one of the two windows out to the front. If I stand on my tiptoes I can see down the mountain and out to the coast, with the ocean, all blue and grey and crazy-enormous. I scan the line where the town meets the beach and then I see the tiny harbour, just the size of a pin-prick from here. It's peaceful. Glorious.

Liam and Gabby would love it.

I rummage in my bag for my phone but when I pull it out and turn it on, error messages come up. No service. I turn it on and then off again, just to check, but there's nothing. I'm frustrated, trying to figure out if it's some button I need to press when I hear a voice.

"Are you ready?"

Grandma's back. Her head is stuck around my door and she's smiling. Like she's amused.

"Um," I say. "I was just..." and I show her my phone.

"Oh, I'm so sorry," she says. "One of the tiny drawbacks of living up here is no mobile access. I think it's because we're so close to the escarpment. We're just in some kind of dead spot for some reason."

I look at my phone and then back at her. Disappointed.

"When we go into town you can check your messages," she says. "That's what I always do."

I drop the phone onto the bed. "Okay," I say. "I just wanted to show my friends the view."

"You must be hungry," she says. "I've got some lunch."

We eat salad sandwiches on the verandah in the sun. The munching keeps us silent but I'm glad. Even though Grandma is super-nice, the fact is I'm going to be here for a full two weeks. Which is a pretty long time. Honestly? I'm a bit nervous that we won't find enough to talk about. Or, worse, that I'm going to say the wrong thing. Do I mention Mum? Will she get upset if I ask about Dad? Maybe I should just stick to gardening. At least that would be safe. And I can think of a zillion questions I could ask her on the topic, mostly about kikuyu grass and good ways to get rid of it.

I swallow my last mouthful and clear my throat but I'm too slow. Grandma gets there first. And she's jumping right in.

"You know what the elephant in the room is, right?" she says.

I think I may have misheard. "Wait, what?" I say.

"Do you know what the phrase, 'the elephant in the room' means?" she asks again. She's grimacing. Awkwardly.

"Um, I think so," I say.

"It means, well, the thing that everyone knows you need to talk about, that nobody talks about and everyone just ignores," she explains.

I nod. *Okay.*

"So, we probably need to talk about some elephants," she says. "And then we can just get on with having a good time together. What do you think?"

I have no idea what I think. Do people actually do this? Talk about the big stuff straight up? What if we all get upset or offended? Will I have to go home?

"What do you think?" she asks again. *Agh. She actually wants an answer.*

I give her one. "Oh, like, okay."

Grandma takes a deep breath.

"I'm so happy to see you here, Jazmine. I'm so glad your mum rang me. I'm so glad you wanted to come. And I want you to know you can ask me anything. I might not necessarily want to answer it, but I will. And I'll tell you the truth. Promise."

I sit for a moment. Overwhelmed. Even though Grandma says everything's okay, she seems a bit tense. I'm not really sure I can totally trust her. Yet. Of course I have questions. Probably more than she can handle. But

I'll have to go slowly. Test the waters. My voice is small and for some reason I half turn away as I'm speaking.

"Do you have any pictures of Dad?"

Grandma's arms lose their stiffness and she lets go of her breath like she's relaxing. She stands up and reaches for me to do the same. "Come on, I'll show you."

I follow her into her room and watch as she opens the door to her walk-in closet. On a small shelf just in front of her are two photos in frames. She picks up the first one.

"I think this is my favourite photo ever of him." She holds the frame out to me and I take it tentatively. From behind the glass a very young man, much younger than I remember, with ruffled hair, wearing a crumpled t-shirt beams up at me. I get a shock.

"He looks just like you," I say, looking up at Grandma. There are the same blue eyes, the same crease of a smile. Even their ear lobes are identical.

"I was going to say he looks like you," Grandma says. She holds the picture next to my face and points me to the mirror. "Look."

I look, and I'm astounded. There, in my face, is my dad's smile, his teeth and his nose. I hold a hand over the top half of my face so I can compare our mouths and chins.

"You see?" says Grandma, grinning. "When you got off the bus today, I couldn't believe my eyes. I knew you always looked similar to him, but it's even more now."

I give a tiny laugh. *Who would have known?* "I always thought I was way more like Mum," I say, but then I realise whose name I've mentioned. "I mean..."

"It's okay," says Grandma. She can see I feel awkward. "You don't have to worry."

I pull in my lips and clench them under my teeth. Strange how when someone says you don't have to worry, you worry anyway.

"Who's the other picture?" I ask. "In there, I mean." I wave my hand towards the closet.

Grandma screws up her nose at me and shrugs. "Well," she says, "You might know her." She picks up the second photo and passes it to me. "Such a little cutie."

For a second I don't realise who the blonde haired baby is staring out of the frame but when I glance back at Grandma's face, I know. It's me. Grandma, who hasn't seen me for four years, keeps my baby photo in her cupboard.

There are no words. I put the picture down and smile at her. She beams back and then she bounces gently on the bed next to me.

"Two weeks, hey?" she says. "Two whole weeks. We're going to have some adventures."

chapter 14

First, we eat.

I'm not sure if Grandma thinks that eating is an adventure but trying things like goat's cheese and weird paté doesn't come up much in my normal life. For the first few days we spend a couple of hours of gardening in the morning and then we head out to literally every single different café and restaurant in town.

Grandma orders something different every time.

I'm the person who looks for the same meal on every menu (totally chips, schnitzel and salad) but she's like, "Oooh, what's that?" to the waiter and, "Okay, aragula/rocket/other weird herbs and vegetables. Sounds exciting! I'll have it."

My mouth tingles and my brain explodes at practically every meal. A few times I attempt to stick to my usual but Grandma gives me a look from across the table.

"Really?" she says. "But have you ever before eaten baked root vegetables in a balsamic dressing, with proscuitto?" And she lifts one eyebrow so high that I have to try not to laugh.

"No," I say. "I haven't."

"Well, then," she says. "It just might be the next love of your life. But you'll never know unless you try it."

When we get our meals she wants to share hers with me as well as try mine, so I push my plate into the middle of the table and gingerly take a few forkfuls of hers.

"What do you love?" she asks. "On the plate. What do you love?"

The question stops me, every time. I have to think. Definitely not avocado or zucchini. I don't know why anyone would want to eat them. But I do love a tiny hit of bacon. I'm starting to taste the beauty in tomatoes and there was one home-made mayonnaise we tried that opened my eyes wide and made my mouth water for more.

"What do *you* love?" I ask her back one day. We're having a late lunch in an open air café opposite the beach. The sun is golden and the sky is the deepest blue I've ever seen. When the waves toss over, the white foamy edges sparkle in the light.

"What do *I* love?" she says. She laughs. "Honestly? I love it when *you* try something new. It's like I'm tasting it for the first time all over again."

"Yeah, but you still like avocado, though," I say.

"True," she says. "But I'm holding out hope that you'll be convinced yet."

One night she makes me put my best clothes on and takes me out to a restaurant on a pier. It's all nautical stuff, old wood and waiters in boat uniforms. We eat our dinner. I share my grilled fish with her and she makes me try oysters, which I don't recommend. Slimy. And then a band comes to the stage and sets up. Two guitarists and one of those huge, standing double bass things.

"I saw these guys at a festival down the coast last year," says Grandma, leaning over to me so I can hear her better. "I think they're really good."

I nod and watch as they get started. I love the way the bass player is just slapping the strings and bobbing with the beat. All the musicians have their eyes shut for different bits as they play. I watch them carefully. I know that feeling, of disappearing into another space, of being overtaken by something else. But I didn't know you could do it with music too.

Grandma grabs my hand.

"Come on," she says. "Let's dance."

Dance? I pull back against her.

"Um, no thanks," I say, almost squishing my bottom into my chair as if that might create some kind of glue that will stop me ever getting up.

"Why not?" says Grandma. "The music is great!"

I look out at the empty dance floor and shake my head again.

Grandma lets go of me. "Okay," she says. "But I will."

She trots out to the dance floor in her orange shoes and turquoise jacket and begins to sway and groove with the music. I scrounge down as low as I can on my chair. *Embarrassment, much!* I have to cover my eyes and hide my face to stop from seeing the rest of the restaurant looking at her and laughing.

After a couple of minutes my neck is getting a crick in it from hiding away. I have to come up for a stretch. And maybe some fresh air as well. I take a breath and turn my neck from side to side. Some people are still sitting at their tables but others are moving over to the dance floor. It suddenly strikes me.

No-one else thinks Grandma is embarrassing.

The idea is astounding.

So astounding, in fact, that I drop my hands to beside my chair and take a good look around me. Grandma is still dancing. But no one is watching her. No one is judging her. No one is laughing at her. In fact, other people are heading out to dance with her.

I put my hands on the table but no one notices. People keep eating, talking, dancing. I stretch them up over my head and yawn. Loudly.

Nothing.

The waiters deliver meals and drinks and walk on by. I stand up. I even jiggle from side to side. And no one notices. It's as though I'm invisible but in a totally different way from how I used to be. Before, I made myself small. I took up no space. I looked away from the world. This time I'm looking at it. I'm taking up space. I'm confident.

And it doesn't matter.

People just don't think that much about me. But I don't think it in a sad way. It's more a feeling of being free. Loose. Exciting.

I take a step away from the table. Just a little one, but it feels huge. Then I take another step and then another and another until finally I'm standing at the edge of the dance floor, just looking at my grandmother, dancing and happy and light. She sees me, stops and smiles. And then she holds out her hand to me, and I take it and step onto the smooth wooden surface and start to move, just a little at first, because I'm shy, but then with bigger and bigger movements until we're both dancing and smiling at each other with delight, and then losing ourselves in the vibrations of the beat coming up through the floor because it's there, and we can, and we are both completely alive.

Later, in the car, in the dark, on the way home, Grandma says, "Your dad loved dancing, you know. He was good at it too."

"I didn't," I say, thoughtfully. "Know, that is."

We sit quietly in our seats as the car flashes past the street lights. The dashboard is lit up in orange, reflecting off Grandma's big, amber necklace.

"I don't know much about him," I say into the dark. "I mean, I do, because he was my dad, but things like dancing, and other stuff he liked, I don't know that much about."

Grandma looks ahead into the road. She turns the corner that leads up the mountain and then the street lights peter out and everything is dark. I look out of the window and realise I can see stars. Not just a few; a whole sky of them.

"He loved dancing, sport, surfing," Grandma says. "Anything where he could move. I could hardly ever get him to sit down when he was a little boy. He drove his teachers crazy at school. I tried to get him to learn the violin when he was eight but he lasted about three weeks before everyone was tearing their hair out."

I laugh. "That's funny."

"It was. Well. Kind of. It ended up that every weekend I'd have to take him on a huge bushwalk or go to the beach. Something really energetic to do together just so he wouldn't tear the place apart." There's a smile in Grandma's voice. "And in the end I loved it as much as he did."

"Did he love gardening?" I say. I'm nervous about the answer. For some reason I want it to be 'yes'.

"Definitely not." Grandma laughs. "I'm afraid the gardening thing skipped him over. You've got it from me, not from him. Waiting for flowers to grow was just too slow for Matt."

Matt. The name jars in my ears. *I called him Dad.*

"It's so funny to think that we both knew him, but in such different ways," I say. "And Mum too."

There's a silence. The stars seem to grow bigger; the darkness blacker. I think of elephants sitting in the back seat and I take a deep breath and ask one of the questions I've wanted to ask since I arrived.

"Do you miss him?" I say, all in one flurry, and then I freeze, with my breath all huddled up in my chest.

In the reflection of the dash lights I see something small creep onto Grandma's cheek. It's shiny and orange and bright. And then I realise. It's a tear.

"Oh, I'm so sorry." I say, hurriedly. "I shouldn't have asked that. I don't want to make you upset. Sorry, sorry."

Grandma says nothing for a few seconds and the small fear inside me turns into a much bigger one. Finally, she nods, almost to herself, and then pulls the car over onto the shoulder of the road. The engine is still running but we're not moving. She turns to me and I can see not just one tear, but a line of them from eye to nose to the top of her mouth.

"Don't apologise, Jaz," she says. "Yes. I miss him. I miss him so much." Her shoulders shake and her voice disappears for a second. She bends her head down and a small pool of wet appears on the gear stick, glimmering in the moonlight.

"When your baby dies..." Her voice chokes and she stops talking. She wipes her nose on her sleeve. "Ugh. Pretend you didn't see that, okay?"

She takes a deep breath, straightens her shoulders and looks forward into the road. "You can't get over your child dying," she says. She sounds strong. "A child should never die before their mother. I almost think it's easier for a wife to lose a husband, and, don't take this wrong, for a child to lose a parent—sometimes. But a mother to lose her baby is, well, it's hell." She spits the last word out.

A car rushes past, its lights catching the canopy of trees above us, then dying away, red and small in the distance. The aftershock of its energy shudders through our seats.

Grandma shakes her head and turns back to me, her hand on the gear stick.

"Never apologise for asking questions," she says. "I'm glad you asked me. Not many people do. Most people want to avoid the topic. They get scared when someone cries."

I'm not sure what to say, so I twist my hands together. "Oh."

"I'm okay," she says. "Mostly. I went from crying every day for months back then to now having just a couple of days a year when I'm not okay. The rest of the time, I choose to do the things that remind me that I'm still alive. Matt would have liked that."

I want to ask more. I want to talk about Mum. Find out why they haven't spoken since it all happened. But for some reason I can't do it. Something is holding me back. Maybe it's the fact that Grandma hasn't actually said Mum's name the whole time I've been here. It's not a big thing. But it's enough to let me know that things are delicate. Touchy. I push the elephant back into its seat and click the seatbelt.

Not now.

Grandma puts her indicator on and we pull out onto the road again. The trees close in above us, shielding the sky and making a tunnel.

"I love this bit," Grandma says. She speeds the car up a little. "It feels like we're driving into a fairytale."

I nod. It's weird. Even a little spooky with the trees blocking out the sky. But then it's over as we turn a corner and then I gasp because down below us, at the bottom of the mountain, are lights. It *is* a fairytale, twinkling and dazzling at our feet. Grandma turns into her driveway and we sit in the car, looking out at the lights below and the stars above. The moon leaves a silver track on the water and, way out to the horizon, tiny ships twinkle orange beacons.

"It's incredible, isn't it?" she says. "Just laid out there, in front of us."

I nod again. "Amazing."

"See the water?" Grandma asks. "Out there, in the ocean?"

"Yes," I say.

"That's where we're going tomorrow."

chapter 15

A ship in a harbour is safe, says Grandma's poster. *But that is not what ships are built for.*

Our 'ship' is more of a boat and quite a small one, really, as boats go. At least, compared to all the other boats tied up at buoys in the little, stone-walled harbour at one end of the beach.

"Can't we go on that one?" I say to Grandma, pointing to a wooden fishing boat with a two storey cabin. "Or what about that one?" I show her a modern cruiser with black tarpaulins pulled tight across the deck. "They look safer."

Grandma laughs. "I'm afraid Adrian doesn't have a hundred thousand dollars to spend on a boat. But his is perfectly safe."

Grandma's friend Adrian waves to us from the deck of his boat. It's actually pretty cute. The bit that sits in the water is painted blue, the deck part is white and then there's a plain timber shelter and a couple of windows to protect the steering wheel. The wind changes direction and the boat turns around slowly. I can see a little trapdoor in the shelter, and the name of the boat painted in gold on the back.

Invincible.

Really?

"I'll come and get you," yells Adrian and Grandma gives him the thumbs up. She's wearing jeans, a red and white striped top and a pair of red canvas sneakers. I'm way more boring, with plain khaki shorts, an oversized white t-shirt and a terrible pair of Crocs that Mum hates but they just keep going and going, no matter what I do to them.

Adrian hops into a tiny row boat and slowly cuts his way through the water towards us. I'm doubtful we'll all fit, and the water isn't far from the edges of the boat when both Grandma and I get in, squashed up together on the little back bench. We make it, though, and get ourselves and the picnic lunch Grandma has packed into the *Invincible*, with only a few salty splashes on our shoes.

"It's wobbly," I say, feeling the movement of the water under the deck of the boat. "Should I sit down?"

"It's fine," says Adrian. He has a big clear voice, like he's been shouting over the noise of the waves for years. "Just don't run around or make extreme movements."

I sit, awkwardly, on the edge of a bench at the back, adjusting my arms over the lifejacket Adrian hands me and carefully putting on my sunscreen. I got burned with Liam at the beach a few weeks ago and the blisters and the peeling were terrible. *Liam.* With cream-smeared hands I feel around for my phone in Grandma's bag. When I check my messages I leave white prints on the screen. I've been looking for something, anything, from

Gabby every time we've come into town, but there's still nothing. Liam has texted me a couple of times and I've sent back short replies with smiley faces all through them.

Sorry, can't txt. Grandma's out of range, and I only get about 5 mins per day. Miss you. (:

Beach is great. Eating out today. Having good holidays? (:

Going on a boat tomozz. Gotta go. Can't chat. (:

There's nothing from him today. Maybe he's gone away with his family for the weekend. His dad was coming back from the US in the middle of the holidays so they might have decided to do something.

The dull roar of the engine interrupts my phone gazing. I put it away and settle back. There's a faint thud, thud, thud in my chest. First time on a boat. I tell myself a few nerves are normal, try to take some deep breaths and act relaxed. Grandma seems perfectly happy. She's standing up under the little shelter, chatting away to Adrian, who's laughing and pointing at different things like he's showing her something.

They seem close. My eyes flash wide for a millisecond with the thought. I'll have to watch them. Carefully.

But that will be later. Right now I'm watching Adrian motor the little boat out of the harbour, past the high stone walls and the concrete blocks, past the beach and the park with the swings and slides and little kids with their mums, through the green and red channel markers which stick out of the water like wet, painted telegraph poles with hats on. There's a white trail of foam behind us, small at first, but as Adrian revs up the engine and goes faster, it gets bigger and wider and more and more hungry.

Grandma looks back at me. She's hanging on to the windscreen in front of her, her hair blowing back from her head. She lifts her eyebrows and smiles as if to say, "You okay?"

I'm clinging to the wooden seat with both hands, my feet pressing so firmly into the deck that it feels like I'm about to put down roots and become a tree. I nod back and smile bravely. "Okay."

There's no point talking. I wouldn't be able to hear anything over the engine roar and the slap of waves and the rush of wind anyway. I shut my eyes to see if I can close out some of the panic in my chest but salt gets in my nose, my hair whips around my face and water splashes my arm. I loosen my grip with one hand to wipe it away and then I realise something.

I haven't died. Or fallen overboard.

I loosen the other hand, just slightly. *Still not dead.*

I prise my feet up from the boards of the deck and nothing happens. I don't tip backwards and the boat doesn't sink. It just keeps going, rushing, bouncing on the water, whisking through the swell.

Actually, this is pretty awesome.

I shift position and look around me. The sky is as blue as I've ever seen it. So is the ocean. It's like the two of them are reflecting off each other in one of those mirrors against a mirror, that shows you yourself to infinity. I'm getting wet, but I don't mind it. It's… I search around my head for the right word. It pops right into my brain.

Exhilarating. Mr Southwell in English would be proud of me.

A random thought pops up. *I could drag my hand in the water.* It's quickly beaten down by a more sensible thought. *Um, no, because... sharks.* But it comes back again, fighting. *Do you really think a shark would even notice two fingers going at the speed of light on the top of the water?* I'm convinced, and recklessly shift over to the side of the bench, lay over the edge of the boat and drop my hand into the water.

Immediately, I'm on a rollercoaster. My hand is tossed around, battered and pulled by the water. I have to focus to keep it firm in the wash and then I feel the entire strength of the ocean pushing past it, fighting it. My breath is coming harder and faster but it's because everything is amazing and crazy and strong.

The sun beats on my face and shoulders and the blue and the spray and the breeze overtake me and I realise that I'm having more fun than I ever imagined. Nothing matters, not even silent friends or sulky boyfriends, not elephants in back rooms, not even fear or panic, when you're out on the water in a boat with some serious speed.

When we're stopped for lunch, bobbing and swaying close to a cove and cliff face, I ask Adrian a question.

"Did you name this boat?" My voice makes its way through stuffed baby red peppers and sushi rolls. (Grandma's choice, not mine.)

"Sure did," he says. "I bought her probably ten years ago, repainted her and gave her a new name."

"Why did you pick it?" I say.

"The boat?"

"No. The name."

"Invincible?" he asks.

"Yeah," I say, "I mean, it's cute and it goes fast, but it seems a bit of an exaggeration. Maybe for one of those bigger ones…" My voice lags a little. I've just realised I sound rude. "Sorry," I say.

"It's okay," he says, frowning slightly. "Fair question. I actually knew the old owner of the boat, you see. Before I bought her, I used to take her out fishing."

I must look confused, because he quickly explains. "I didn't buy the owner. I bought the boat. We call boats 'she'."

I nod, like, *of course I knew that* and he keeps going.

"Once I took her out and the weather looked fine but it turned bad pretty fast and before I knew it I was in the middle of a storm."

"Really?" says Grandma. "When was that?"

"About 12 years ago. Do you remember that mini-cyclone thing that did all that damage to the fire station?"

"Truly?" squawks Grandma. "Not that one!"

Adrian nods and shrugs. "Yep. It was quick and it was serious and we were out in the middle of it. Just me and this girl." He slaps the wooden side affectionately with his hand.

"What happened?" I ask, looking around at the flat water and fluffy clouds and imagining it all turning to grey chaos.

"I hadn't gone that far. It had only been half an hour

since I left the harbour," he said. "But it took us over two and a half hours to get back. In the end, I had to turn off the engine to save fuel and I went into the hold, down there in that trapdoor, and sat braced up against it, just waiting."

"You must have been terrified," I said. I look at the tiny space under the front part of the boat and imagine myself in there, curled up, scared and crying.

"I was actually more sick," he said. "The waves were huge and the boat was tipping around like anything."

"Were you worried?" asks Grandma.

"Yes," he says, but thoughtfully. "A bit. I mean, of course boats sink. Waves can smash you up. People drown." He looks down at the wood under his feet. "But I actually wasn't that scared. I knew that this boat was really well made. She's strong and she's sturdy. She'd been through storms before, she was well looked after, and I figured she could do it again."

"What happened?" I say. I'm on the edge of my seat.

"Storm passed," says Adrian, tipping his head to the side. His smile relaxes me. It's calm and quiet. "The weather will always change eventually. I started up the engine again and headed home. She had a bit of damage, of course, but it wasn't anything I couldn't fix and after a new paint and a bit of bodywork, she was ready to go out again."

"So you named her…"

"… Invincible, yes," says Adrian, finishing my sentence. "I thought she deserved a strong name after what she'd been through. But I call her 'Vincey' for short."

I screw up my nose. "That's a terrible name."

Adrian laughs and so does Grandma. "I'd like to see you come up with something better," he says and looks at the sushi Grandma's put out in front of him. "Did you bring any real food? Bread? Ham? Jam, maybe?" He grins at her, she makes an amused face back, hands him a punnet of blueberries and I laugh out loud. Even the boat, *Vincey*, seems to be smiling in the sunshine. I take a bite of my own sushi and look out to the horizon. Somehow, I just can't imagine a storm coming up so quickly on such an amazing day.

chapter 16

I can't shake this feeling that something's going on back at home. I've been at Grandma's for 11 days now but I've heard from Liam maybe three times at most. And that was last week. There's been nothing since the middle weekend of the holidays. At home he texts me every day or even more. When you add it to the fact that Gabby's apparently just disappeared off the planet, I'm feeling a bit weird. Dislodged, dislocated. Other 'dis' words too, I'm sure, if I could think of them. Having actual friends is still such a new thing for me that I'm not sure what's going on. Or what I can do about it. Is this kind of stuff even normal?

It doesn't seem to bother me in the day when I'm out with Grandma, doing things and going places, but at night when my hearing aids are out and I'm muffled in my own brain, going to sleep, I run through all kinds of scenarios. *Liam hates me, or he thinks I hate him. Gabby's never going to speak to me again because she thinks I made her get in a fight. What did I do wrong? How can I make it right?*

The evil ghouls in my dreams have taken a little break

And then there's a rumble in my heart. It's the elephants again.

I have to speak.

"Why haven't you ever come to see me and Mum?" My question rattles out like bits of gravel being swirled out of a bucket. It sits between us like rubble. *Gah. I'm not getting any better at saying things politely.*

There's a silence. I shiver and I can't tell if it's because I've made us cold or because there's a breeze coming up. Nothing happens for a minute and I'm just about to open my mouth and try to make things better, *apologise*, when Grandma stands up.

Her face is tight.

"I'm sorry I told you to ask whatever you wanted," she says. "I'm sorry. There are just some things…" She shakes her head. "I can't talk about… I just can't." She turns away from me and I can feel tears starting in my eyes. Around me, suddenly, the air is heavier.

"Excuse me," she says, tense and harsh. "I need to be on my own for a bit," and she turns abruptly and walks off, back down the path into the bush.

I'm light headed and disbelieving. My hands are clenching themselves automatically, on-off, on-off and my legs are feeling wobbly. I crane my head to follow Grandma, not daring to get up and go with her, but terrified to stay here on my own. The cliff drop seems closer, the rocks darker and the view, instead of being full of delight now appears to be reaching out swirly hands towards me, trying to suck me in. In the distance a cloud has appeared. I wasn't mistaken before. The sky really is getting grey.

We're going to have a storm.

Frozen, I sit on my rock like a statue on its base. I don't know how long I'm there. Ten minutes? Twenty? Time could be zooming by or standing still, I wouldn't really know. But Grandma hasn't come back, even though my eyes are trained towards the way she went, willing her to emerge from the trees, all smiles again. "Jaz! It was a joke!"

Yeah, right.

My stomach is telling me it's time to eat but I don't want to dig in the bags for food without Grandma. She'll think I'm rude, starting without her. And I am rude. Rude to ask questions. Rude to want to know. Rude and ridiculous to think that when someone, even someone who's your grandma, says you can be honest, you really can.

I can't bear it any more. I have to find her. I run back to the path, into the bush, through the trees. Twenty or 30 metres in, in a small clearing I stop and look around. No sign of Grandma. Surely she hasn't started down the mountain without me? I'll have to look again.

"Grandma!" I shout. "Grandma!" But it's a pointless exercise. Am I going to be able to hear her if she yells back? Still, maybe she'll at least know that I'm looking for her.

I head back towards the rocks again. Maybe she's headed back there and is looking for me. My head is going left and right, back and forth, sweeping the bush for clues. And then I find one. It's a tiny, half-beaten path going off the right. I'm guessing it leads to a flat place I saw on the edge of the cliff drop.

It's a squeeze through bushes and an obstacle course over dead branches and vines.

"Grandma!" I call. "Grandma! Are you here?"

And then I hear just a tiny sound, so shrill it could almost be a bird call. "Aaz."

I call again. "Grandma?" And I hear it again, just a little louder. "Aaaz."

And then I'm running, as fast as I can, tripping over wood and leaves and scratching my face on branches towards the sound, towards Grandma. It must be her. It is her. I have to find her.

And then, rounding a corner, I do.

She's lying on the path on her side, her hair fanned out over a rock. She's holding her arm and crying and shouting, "Jaz, Jaz."

My Grandma is hurt. And I kneel down, crying and sobbing and trying not to hurt her as I hug her.

"It's okay," I say, tears running down my face. "It's okay. I'm here."

chapter 17

We hug for a moment before Grandma grabs my arm.

"I think I'm injured," she says, pulling me towards her so I can see her face. There are lines on it I haven't seen before; a look of terror, or horror. Something I don't recognise. Her voice wavers and goes small. "I'm so sorry. So sorry."

I sit back on my heels and brush a leaf off her hair. "It's not your fault," I say. "It's okay," but she shakes her head from side to side.

"No. I'm sorry. I was hurt."

"It doesn't matter," I say. I'm not quite sure what she means. "It's not important. But we need to get you up. Is your arm hurting?"

Grandma nods and winces. I chew my lips and think back to old episodes of *The Famous Five* Mum used to play for me on the video machine before we finally threw it out. "I loved them," she always said. "Especially George and Timmy. You will too."

To be honest, I wasn't sure about the Five. They weren't like any kids I'd ever met, always getting themselves into crazy situations. On the other hand,

Grandma nods. "Ambulance. Fire. Whoever. The emergency number. They'll know who to send. Just remember: it's Trembler's Rocks."

I nod. There are butterflies in my stomach and my mouth is dry. I pull out a water bottle and the phone to take with me.

"Hopefully I'll be back in two hours," I say. "It won't be long."

Grandma nods. She looks tired. "I'll just stay here," she says, with a tiny smile. It's her little joke. "I won't go anywhere."

I kiss her on the cheek, and then again on the top of the head and then I wait just a tiny second, still hesitating, before George from the Famous Five pokes me in the back and tells me to get going, I'm wasting time.

The path is just as rough going down as it is coming up. I'm going so fast that I fall over a couple of times, grazing my hands on the rocks, before I tell myself sternly to be careful; I can't afford an injury as well. My muscles hurt again, but the pain doesn't take over my head like it did on the way up. I've got more important things to think about. Every ten minutes I open the phone and check for reception but the little bars stay dark and silent.

Help me, help me, help me, I say, over and over to whoever is listening. *Let Grandma be okay. Let me find some help. I don't know what to do.* The path is a mess of roots and branches and rotten logs and I pick my way across them as fast as I can, heading down, down, down the hill, further and further away from Grandma. I'm vaguely aware that I'm hungry and vaguely aware that

I'm cold but none of it matters. I just have to get down, get help and get back.

After three quarters of an hour the path flattens out again and then I start to run, panting and coughing. A slow jog is all I can manage after about five minutes. I'm definitely not fit enough for finding my way out of crazy situations. Eventually I have to stop, panting, my hands on my knees and head down.

And then I see it.

The phone has reception.

I press the numbers quickly and sloppily, almost getting them wrong, and then hold the phone hungrily to my ear. There's a ring, ring, space, ring, ring, and then, relief! A voice. Saying hello. Asking how she can help me.

I stumble out my words, still panting from the running and I'm talking so quickly that she almost can't understand me.

"Please slow down. What is your emergency?"

"My grandma is injured. She's at the top of the mountain, you know, Trembler's Rocks?"

"What road is that on?" says the voice.

"Road?" I say. Panic fills my stomach. "I have no idea what road it is. I came here with my grandma. She drove. I'm just 14. I'm not even from here."

"It's okay," says the voice. "You'll be okay. Take a deep breath and we'll go through it again. I'm going to get you some help."

It takes maybe six minutes before we work out where exactly we are, what sort of injuries Grandma has and how they can get to us.

"It's going to be over an hour before someone can get up there," says the woman. "Maybe even two. And with the storm coming, it may take longer. Because there are just two of you, I want you to go back to your Grandma and stay with her. Keep her warm. Give her a drink. Can you do that?"

"Okay," I say. "I can." My stomach goes tight again. "But will you come? Are you sure?"

"Totally sure," she says. "Someone's on their way."

I hang up the phone. For a second I want to cry but I hold it back. This isn't the time. I've got to get back to Grandma.

chapter 18

By the time I drag myself to the top of Trembler's Rocks, for the second time in one day, I'm trembling, myself, with pain and tiredness. Plus I'm hungry, plus I'm cold, plus I've emptied my water bottle. I'll have to check and see if we have another one.

Oh yes, and there's thunder and lightning crashing and smashing around my head. It started halfway up the really steep bit and I nearly jumped when I heard the first roll. It's huge and booming and sparkly in the sky. Thunder and lightning are fine when you're inside looking out. When you're outside wanting to be in and home and safe and warm, it's not so good.

When I finally stumble back down the little breakaway path towards Grandma I find her sleeping, covered with the picnic blanket. I throw myself on the ground, exhausted and wobbly and just lie there for a while. When I finally move again, reaching out for another drink and maybe some chocolate, my legs and arms and feet feel like they're not quite mine, not quite in my control. I suck greedily at another juice box and stuff the sugar in my mouth in one go. I want to eat more but I'm worried we might have to be here for a while. *George wouldn't eat it all now*, I think and decide to ignore the pains in my empty belly.

There's a massive crack of thunder and Grandma's eyes jerk awake. For a half second she looks scared and uncertain and I have a flash and understanding that she is old. My grandmother is an old woman. I don't really know what to do with that.

She looks around and then sees me sitting just away from her. A smile of relief covers her face.

"Oh sweetheart. You did it!"

"They're coming to get us, Grandma. It won't be straight away, and they'll probably have to get you down in a stretcher, so you'll have to hang tight for a bit longer, okay?"

She nods and I can see tears welling. Her good hand reaches from under the blanket to catch my own and her grip is wobbly.

"Thank you, Jaz." She shakes her head. "Thank you. I'm so sorry."

"The woman on the phone said I had to keep you warm," I say. "And to give you a drink." I reach for a bottle of water. "You have to have some. She said so."

Grandma takes a sip and just as she puts the bottle down, there's another explosion of thunder and a *zzizt* of lightning. I look up at the tree trunk she's leaning against. I'm not an expert on storms but even I know that trees and lightening don't mix.

"I think we'll have to move."

I hoist Grandma up, wincing and whimpering and half-drag, half-carry her to a spot under a straggly looking bush.

"We're going to have to sit on the packs," I say. "And we can cover ourselves with the blanket."

It's hard and uncomfortable and boring to wait, and my legs and arms are aching, especially with Grandma leaning on me. When the rain finally comes down I think I just might possibly die from cold and wet and misery, not to mention the very annoying, pointy rock that seems to be lodged under my bottom. But I have to stay strong. Grandma is depending on me.

What would George do? I think to myself, over and over. *What would George do if she was wet and cold and miserable?* But there's only one answer. George would stick it out. She'd hug her dog and sit close to her friends and shut her eyes and find every single, tiny bit of strength inside her to keep going.

So I put one arm around Grandma and one arm around my own knees, shut my eyes and think of all my favourite things; my plants, my journal. Mum and Gabby. Liam's eyes and the way the twins do everything together. I think of Dad's smile and the feeling I always had when he hugged me. I think of Grandma and the things she's made me eat, and dancing with no one looking. I think of Adrian and the sparkle of the ocean and the bounce of his little boat, Vincey, and how she made it through a storm as well.

If she can do it, so can I.

We sit and sit and sit, Grandma and I, dripping water and shivering and waiting. And then, all in one arc of light, the rain stops, the sky clears and Grandma hears something.

"I think they're coming," she says, her voice trembling and her chin jutting out like she's trying to catch a sound. "I can hear voices."

I stand up, trying not to fall over. A lot of sitting with super-tired legs makes for a wobbly start. "I'll go and see."

I dash over the roots and rocks again, trying not to slip on the mud that the storm has created. In the late afternoon light, I can see through the bush, down the main path. A rescue party. Four men and a woman in bright yellow overalls. They've got backpacks and what looks like a stretcher.

My wobbly legs are forgotten. We're going to get out of here. I dance up and down, waving wildly. "Hi, over here. Hello. It's me. We're here."

Nothing's over until much, much later. First we have to get down the mountain with Grandma on a stretcher. She's embarrassed and apologising until the woman tells her it's fine, just to relax, that these things happen, and we make our way slowly down to the bottom where there's an ambulance waiting to take us both to the hospital. Even then it isn't over. We still have to wait and wait and wait while doctors do tests and take x-rays and check bloods. Grandma gives me Adrian's number and he comes right over with a hamburger for me in a large paper bag, stays until everything is sorted out and then promises to pick us up and take us wherever we need to go whenever we need to go there.

Grandma has to stay in overnight with a broken wrist and sprained ankle *and* knee and I stay with her in the room, curled up and snoozy in an armchair, ignoring all the nurses who come in and take her blood pressure and give her pills in the middle of the night. I'm so stiff from my 20 kilometre walk up and down a mountain twice that I can hardly move in the morning but a kind hospital person brings me a tray of breakfast with Grandma's.

Grandma's face is still white but she looks better than she did yesterday. And she's hungry.

"So," she says, looking down at the tray and then up at me and grinning. "What do you love?"

"Plain white toast," I say. "With jam." I take an enormous, deliberate bite in front of her. She makes an amusing disgusted face but eats hers just as quickly as me.

"When you're hungry, it all goes down," she says. "I'd prefer eggs with a hollandaise sauce, but at least we're not eating bush tucker at the top of Trembler's Rocks."

My eyes get big in alarm. "I wouldn't know what to look for," I say. "Anyway, would you really eat a grub or a spider? Assuming I could catch one of course."

"Maybe." She shrugs. "I'd probably give it a go. Especially if it was the only thing on offer."

"Remind me never to go camping with you," I say and sip my hot chocolate.

She picks up her cup. And then puts it down again.

"I need to apologise to you," she says.

I open my mouth, but she speaks over me. "No, I'm sorry. I'm not very good at this so I'll have to just say it all in one go or I might not do it at all."

I blink a little and sit back in my chair, waiting.

"The truth is, I got upset when you asked me about your mum and you. I know it was unfair of me, I mean,

I told you to ask whatever you wanted to ask and not worry about the elephant in the room and all that."

She takes a sip of her tea and swallows. "When Matt — your dad — died, like I told you, it was absolutely devastating. I was broken up. But even in the middle of all the agony, I felt like… I don't know. Like I'd have to change something." She puts down her cup and shakes her hair around a little.

"It seemed like there were only two choices for me: stay home and cry and then get old and die. Or get out and keep living. I decided that I would do things to be happy. Things like eating out, going dancing, moving house, making new friends."

I nod slowly.

"Your mum was different to me," Grandma says. "She cried all the time. And I got so that I couldn't bear being around all the tears and the sad faces. It made me feel so much worse, almost like I was being suffocated."

She looks up at me. "Sorry. I don't want to upset you." She stares at the wall for a bit. I wait.

"After a little while of this, because we were there together a lot in those months, if you remember, we had a big fight. She said that I wasn't even missing Matt, and I mustn't have loved him. And maybe… well, maybe that was the reason he, you know… took his own life."

She stops for a moment, looks down at her lap and twists her napkin around her fingers.

"I'm sorry. This is probably hard for you to hear," she says.

I don't really know how to answer. I'm listening, but it's almost like it's not me, here in my body, using my ears and my hearing aid and my eyes to read Grandma's lips when she gets quiet. This person, whoever it is, is calmer than I could be, or maybe it's because she just can't feel anything much.

"It's okay," says whoever-is-in-my-body. "It's okay."

Grandma keeps on going. "But I have to be honest. I said terrible things to her too. I told her that she was weak. No spine. No character. I said if she kept crying and crying she'd cry a river that would eventually sweep you away. I told her she'd destroy you. Just like she'd destroyed my son."

A tear trickles down Grandma's cheek, and then another, until her face is as wet as it was in the rain last night. I put my tray down on the floor, leaving the toast half eaten (Grandma was right: white bread tastes terrible after you haven't had it for a while) and go to sit next to her on the bed. All I can think of saying is 'don't cry' but it's such a stupid thing to say that I slap myself over the head in my imagination. Instead I put my arms around my grandmother and just hold her tight, like she needs to be held. She cries for a few minutes, dribbling tears onto my lap, but I let it go. The shorts need to be washed anyway.

Eventually Grandma comes up for air, gasping a little, and wipes her face. I shift my arm and loosen the hug.

"You're an amazing person, Jazmine," she says. "Really. I am proud to have you as my grand-daughter."

Immediately I land in my body again, swamped by a pile of odd-sized emotions. Embarrassment, disbelief, shock and then a very, very warm feeling that starts in my toes and moves up to my heart. I can't stop a smile.

"I'm proud of you too," I say.

"Well, I'm not proud of me," she says, decisive. "I treated your mother badly. And I let my fight with her take over even things like sending you birthday cards. So I treated you badly too. And I'm really sorry. I've missed four whole years with you, and I can't get them back."

"Do you think you meant what you said to Mum?" I ask.

"Do any of us know what we're saying when we're hurt and angry?" she says. "I probably thought I meant it at the time. I certainly wish now I hadn't said it. In the end, I think we just really didn't understand each other. And I was mean."

chapter 19

When we finally get home Adrian checks we're okay and that the fridge has food in it.

"Call me if you need anything," he says. "I can be up here in five minutes."

I nod and wave good bye and walk back into the house where Grandma is propped up on the sofa, her wrist in a cast and her foot on a pillow.

"I think I should call Mum," I say. I'm calm, even though it feels like it could be a dangerous thing to say. "She'd probably want to know what's happened."

Grandma nods. "I think that's a good idea."

"She might want me to go home."

"Whatever you need to do is fine with me, sweetheart. I'll be okay. I've got people who'll help me out."

"I don't want to go," I say. "You know that, right?"

She lowers her head slightly. "Of course."

When I dial the number there's a 'brr, brr', a tiny pause and then Mum's voice, loud and worried. "This isn't your usual time to call, Jaz," she says. "You okay?"

"Yeah," I say. "But Grandma's not."

I know Mum has always been a worrier but I've never heard her go off on the end of a phone before. Once we finally get through the exclamations of *What?* and *Where?* and *You ran how far?* and then limp back into *Are you sure you're okay?* territory, she starts to calm down a bit.

Until she asks me about booking a ticket home early.

"I'm going to stay," I say. She starts in but I talk over her. "No, Mum. I'm going to stay until Saturday, like we planned. Grandma needs me. I want to look after her."

There's a silence on the phone. And then a small voice. "Will you stay there forever?"

"Dont be silly. I'll be back on the weekend."

"Do you even know how to look after someone?" Mum's voice sounds disappointed, almost... bitter?

"I can figure it out," I say.

And I do.

We need to eat so I cook. We need to drink so I make cups of tea and juice. We need to sleep so I put Grandma to bed and take a nap myself. I help Grandma to the bathroom and I tidy up the house.

Day one sorted.

On the second day I help Grandma get to her crutch so she can hobble out to the deck. We slowly edge out through the front door when she says, "I think I can hear a car coming."

I turn to look and, sure enough, coming up the road is a grey hatchback. Just like our car.

As it gets closer I can see the driver. It's a woman. She looks just like Mum.

It is Mum.

My heart leaps at exactly the same time that my stomach freezes. I'm looking at the car and then looking back at Grandma who hasn't recognised her yet. She's still fussing with her crutch, trying to get through the sliding glass doors without sticking the end of it in the frame. My face goes hot and red and my fingers start twitching.

The car, *my* car, pulls off the road and into the drive and I can't even move. Grandma, on the other hand, is walking remarkably well. She's seen the car and is now clumping down the steps, one at a time, onto the gravel. As the car pulls to a stop, she's right there, exactly opposite the driver's side.

The door opens and Mum gets out. She just stands there for a bit at first. Grandma is watching her, waiting, for something. I'm not sure what, but I hope it happens soon because I can't actually breathe. I know what would go down if this was school. Mum would throw the first punch and Grandma would kick back and then the two of them would be surrounded by a mob, yelling and screaming for more.

This isn't school.

Instead, Grandma holds out a hand, just quietly. And Mum takes it. And then the two of them are hugging like they'll never let go, hanging on to each other like people you see on TV who've just survived an earthquake and have found their family again, and then they're crying with tears like fountains out of their eyes, sobbing like the worst, saddest thing in the world has just happened.

I stand and watch, under a blue sky with clouds and shadows and sunshine. I look at my mum and my grandma and then I look out, past them, at the view of the world out there, where life is happening right now, for more people than I can count. Life's happening here for me. And for Mum. And Grandma. I look back at them, still with their arms around each other, and swipe a little tear of my own out of my eye.

Then I walk down the steps.

"Mum, Grandma. Shall I make some tea?"

I make them hot drinks to have on the deck, cold drinks and sandwiches to have inside and then, later, soup and toast for dinner.

"Can I help you?" asks Mum. She's asked me that a few times but each time I've said no. I'm fine, thanks.

"Are you sure?" she says, and I smile.

"It's all good. Just relax."

So she does. At least, she's beginning to, by the end of the day. At first I can see her looking over at me, obviously worrying. I can just about hear the thoughts churning in her head. *Can she do this? Is she okay?* But by the time she's been served fruit for dessert and her third cup of tea for the afternoon, her face is telling a different story. And the story is mostly about Grandma.

The two of them have talked and sat and talked and cried and sat and talked some more. They've looked at photos, they've held hands quietly and they've giggled like nine year olds.

Finally Grandma is tired and white-faced.

"She needs to sleep," I tell Mum. "I'll just put her to bed."

Mum raises her eyebrows and sits back. "Sure."

"Are you ready?" I ask Grandma before I help her out

of her seat. "One, two, three." We stand up together and I help her find her crutch so she can hobble down the hall and into her room, but she's not even looking for them. Instead, she stands as straight as she can, her hand resting on my arm.

"Helen," she says to Mum, her voice nearly breaking. "Your daughter is incredible." Her fingers squeeze my arm and my face gets hot. "She is the bravest young woman I know. She's honest. She's loving. And she's completely, totally, genuine. You have done an amazing job." She half shakes her head. "I want you to know I was completely wrong."

My scalp is burning with so much embarrassment that I'm sure my hair must be turning red as well.

Grandma's voice goes back to normal. "Jaz," she says. "Can you find your mum a towel and some blankets? In the hall cupboard there should be some. See what you can manage."

When I turn off Grandma's light after settling her into bed and come back to the lounge room, Mum is standing at the kitchen bench, looking at the two photos in frames that Grandma brought out before. Dad and me.

I walk up beside her and she turns her head.

"You were so cute," she says. "Look at you."

"I was so young," I say. I gesture to the picture of Dad. "Do you think I look like him? Grandma does."

She tilts her head to one side, thinking. "Sometimes you do. And then sometimes not at all. Maybe, though, you look more like Grandma. I saw it today." She goes quiet.

My voice jerks into the room. "Do you think you guys

will be friends again?" I ask. The question seems to fill the kitchen.

There's a space and then Mum nods. "I think we will," she says.

Later, just before I turn off my light, she knocks on my door in her pyjamas. "You asleep yet?"

I make a face and let her in. "Um, obviously not."

She steps in and looks around. "It's nice in here," she says. "Maybe we need to redecorate at home a bit. I never liked Grandma's style much but maybe it's grown on me. Kind of fresh."

"Adventurous," I say, sitting on the bed. Mum sits beside me and then swings her feet over so she's lying down.

"Especially that," she says, pointing to the print of the boat and the sea. "That's amazing."

I look at the blue and green swirls of water from across the room and imagine myself in that boat, in that ocean, sailing out to somewhere. *Doesn't matter where,* I think to myself. *Just as long as it's out of the harbour.* I think of Vincey, bobbing and puttering along and standing her ground in the middle of a storm and I realise, for the first time in my life, that 'safe' isn't always the most important thing. Living, doing what we're built for, is better. And in that second, I know, more deeply than I've known anything else, that I, Jazmine, want to live.

"I can't believe you ran up and down a mountain twice," says Mum, reaching out for my hand.

"I can't believe it either," I say. "My legs still hurt."

"Mine would have fallen off," she says, and I laugh.

"I'm glad you're here," I say.

"I couldn't not come," she says.

"I know," I say. And I hold her hand.

The next two days are all about getting Grandma to physio, moving things around so she can be more and more independent, and talking to Adrian so he knows how to look after her. She's napping and getting lots of rest but she looks better. I know she's starting to get back to normal when I catch her outside trying to prune a hedge, balancing herself on her crutch.

"No!" I say firmly, but smiling.

She raises one eyebrow. "Just try and stop me."

When I hug her goodbye on Saturday, she holds on to me for longer than I expect.

"You can't go for too long, now," she says. "Now that I have you both back, I need to see you. Next holidays."

"Really?" I say. I'm jumping on the inside.

"Really," she says. "You and me. Lots of cafés. No bushwalks. Deal?"

"Deal."

In the car on the drive home Mum's quiet and so am I.

"Thanks for letting me go," I say.

"Thanks for asking," she says.

"I'm looking forward to going back," I say.

"I'm sure you are," she says.

We sit in silence again until my new, grownup self tries to make conversation.

"So. How were things at home, anyway?"

Mum twists her mouth up a little and tilts her head.

"Things at home?" She pauses a beat. I can see her choosing her words. "Things at home are probably going to be a bit... different."

chapter 20

The only thing that's different is the fact that Mum's moved the sofa to the other side of the living room.

"Is that what you're talking about?" I ask. She shrugs. "Maybe."

I frown slightly and look around the rest of the house and outside.

"You didn't water my garden much," I say, accusingly. The new flowers are drooping and some of the seedlings I put in just before I went away have shrivelled up and died. Luckily I've brought back some cuttings from Grandma's garden.

"I'm so sorry," Mum says. "Really I am. I did it three times but I guess I forgot after that."

"Too many things to think about?" I say. The sarcasm escapes my mouth in a surprising burst. I'm not normally sarcastic. *Why start now?*

To my surprise, Mum looks slightly guilty. "I guess so."

"Like what?" I'm genuinely curious. The sarcasm is gone.

"Oh, just stuff," she says. "People from work." She

turns to me, her face suddenly cheery. "Have you got all your things ready for school tomorrow?"

A shiver goes through my stomach. I catch it and push it into a small space. *Deal with that later.* "I think so. I'll check my shoes and everything." A thought occurs to me. "And I'll have to take my notes on our Science project. Alvin and the other guys will want to get going on it."

Later I text Liam.

Hey, did you have good holidays? I'll have to tell you about my mountain adventure. Has anyone heard from Gabby? Can't wait to see you. Jaz.

I spell out xxx at the end of my name, look at it and then for some reason that I can't understand, go back and delete it before I press Send.

There's an answer soon. Short and simple.

See you tomozz! Xxxxx xxxxxx xxxxx

I put the phone down and away.

Later that night the bad dreams come back. I'm followed by seven foot men with long limbs, leather faces and machetes in their hands. Terrified, I try to run but my feet are stuck and I have to haul myself along with my arms to move.

I wake early, before dawn, scared and tired. But mostly annoyed.

Really? Still? I think. *How long is this going to go on for?*

Going back to sleep is risky. I don't know what kind of monster will be waiting to ambush me. But staying awake will just make me worry about school. Instead I pull out my journal, sadly ignored at Grandma's place, and write. I fill page after page with words and pictures;

descriptions of places, food, people, and, of course, bush tracks and rocks and crazy-vicious lightning bolts.

It helps. When Mum asks how I slept I can say, "I'm okay," instead of, "Sleep? Ha! I need another whole night of it to recover." And then I'm eating and getting dressed and on the bus and pulling up to school, and there, waiting for me like usual, is Liam.

I see him before he sees me. The curl of his hair and the way his shirt hangs on his shoulders make me smile and I'm bounding down the steps and out of the door before he turns around.

"Hi!" I say, and I hug him hard and tight. Maybe he's surprised, or not expecting me because it takes him almost a full second to hug me back. He's stiff; tense, like he wasn't expecting this, but then his arms come out and he pats me on the back.

"Hey." He smiles, but there's something in his eyes.

"You okay?" I say, stepping back. "Have a good holiday?"

He shrugs. "Yeah, sure."

"But really," I say again, eyebrows in a furrow. "You okay?"

There's a flash of annoyance. "Course I am."

"It's just you seem…"

"There's nothing wrong with me," he says. "I'm just annoyed you keep asking."

I go quiet. "Okay. Sorry."

We walk for a bit and then he asks. "Did you miss me?"

"Yeah," I say. "Of course."

He looks to the side. "You didn't message me much."

Immediately I feel guilty. "I'm really sorry, Liam. Honestly, with Grandma, we were like out every day and doing things, and then she had this really bad accident when we were on a hike and I had to call the ambulance and the emergency services and stuff and..."

He hardly seems to listen. "You just could have, though."

A hot feeling spreads from my chest to my forehead and my lungs get tight. I'm sure I'm turning red. "I'm really sorry. I am. Now I feel really bad."

He looks at me, pouts and then shrugs his shoulders. "Hey, it's okay. I'm kind of joking. I'm not serious."

I breathe again and he puts his arm around me. "I missed you heaps," he says in a low voice. "I didn't know what to do without you." My heart skips a beat and the scared feelings disappear.

"So. I forgot to ask. Do you know if anyone heard from Gabby?" I say. "She hasn't answered her phone all holidays."

"Not me," he says. "But maybe the others."

At our table Erin, Olivia and Caitlin are hugging each other. They stop to hug me and air kiss my cheeks. It's something I've learned to get used to in the last few months. Sometimes we even hug when we're going off to different classes. To me it's weird. We're only going to be apart for like, 50 minutes. But since they started doing it I have too.

"Hey, you guys," I say. "Do anything exciting?"

Erin screws up her mouth. "My parents refuse to do anything fun. We just stayed home the whole time. Like, so boring."

Olivia and Caitlin give each other quick looks.

"Beach for three days," says Olivia, and Caitlin continues, "and then home." They take deep breaths at exactly the same time before the words rush out of their mouths in unison: "And we went to Angela's party."

Angela.

I forgot about Angela.

But she hasn't forgotten about me. She's walking over to the table with her friends like she owns the space, arms outstretched and a face like she's seeing her oldest, bestest friend.

"Liam!" she calls, and comes right up to him for a hug. I watch. It's a long one. Longer than necessary? My eyes narrow.

"So good to see you," she says, and her head tips back and to the side with a swish of ponytail. "Can't believe it's only been a week. Seems like forever." She pulls herself away and kisses everyone else.

Everyone except me.

I'm waiting for a hug, or at least a smile, just because she's given one to everyone else, but there's nothing. It's like she hasn't even seen me. Like I'm not even standing here.

"Hey, Angela," I say. My heart is beating but I feel brave. Almost like I felt when I rang for the ambulance. I'm sturdy inside, steadfast. Like a rock. I just want to see how she's going to react; what it's going to be between us.

I know she hears me because there's a flick of something across her face but she ignores me completely. Another rush of courage surges from my feet up to my heart.

"Hey, Angela." I say it again. This time louder.

There's no mistaking it now. Angela is snubbing me. Her eyes go to my face and then deliberately move past me to focus on the twins. "Hey, Caitivia," she says and giggles. "I'm going to call you that now because you were so cute at the party." She turns to the girls around her. "Did you see them? They even sipped their drinks at the same time. Gorgeous."

Caitlin and Olivia smile nervously and join in the laughter. Then they both bend down at the same time to adjust their shoes, realise what they're doing and stand up again, embarrassed. The laughter gets louder and their faces go red.

"Oh, cute. You guys are blushing," says Angela. Her smile looks as genuine as it can possibly be and in that exact second I hate her with all my heart. Why couldn't she have taken a hint from Gabby and stayed away from me after she got slapped? Where is Gabby, anyway?

Everyone's gathered around Angela, including Liam for some reason. No one's even talking to me so I grab my phone out of my bag, find Gabby's number and dial it. Again. Just in case. Maybe she's walking into school right now. Maybe she'll pick it up and tell me she'll be back when her suspension is over. Maybe she'll explain that she dropped her phone in the bath and she's been drying it out for two weeks. In rice. Just like she told me to do once.

I wait for the little 'brrr brrr' noises I'm so used to hearing but they don't come on. Instead, I can't believe my ears. There's a computer-generated woman's voice on the other end.

'*This number has been changed or is no longer in service. Please check the number and dial again.* Click. Beep, beep beep.'

I look at it, puzzled. Did I really dial it wrong? I know Gabby's number, not only in my head but in my fingers too. I do it again, just in case.

But it's the same.

'*This number has been changed or is no longer in service. Please check...*'

I hang up before it cuts me off.

The bell goes for class and Gabby still doesn't turn up. I'm confused. No one has seen her, and now I can't even leave her a message. I have no idea what is going on.

School happens. Classes happen. I go here, I go there, I do maths, I sit through history, I eat my recess and lunch and I disappear to the bathrooms so I don't have to see Angela flirting with Liam.

Last period is drama and a new teacher walks in. "I'm Mrs Brown," she says. "I'm filling in for Miss Fraser. She's away this term on long service leave." My heart sinks. The one person I could have talked to about Gabby, or even about Angela; the one person who would understand, isn't here.

And then I get a note across my desk.

It's from Caitlin, who's trying, harder than I've ever seen, to look innocent. She's working so hard that she actually looks guilty. Next to her, Olivia is on full alert, checking around her like a meerkat I saw at the zoo once. They stand on guard all day, looking for danger.

I'm curious and open the note.

What I read sends my face pale. Makes my breath come short and sharp.

We didn't want to tell you but we thought you should know. At the party Liam and Angela were kissing. A lot.

I push the note away from me and look down at the desk, blinking hard. Trying to compose myself. I have to stay calm; have to find out the facts so I know what I'm dealing with.

Did you see it? I push the note back across the desk. Caitlin takes it, trying hard to be unnoticed.

We both did. We're so sorry, Jaz.

I screw it up tiny and clench my fist around it. I can feel the paper crushing and bending; dying underneath my fingers. This can't be true. Liam is cheating on me? With Angela? It's not possible. He told me he likes *me*. That he'd be there for *me*, no matter what.

And then something gross rises up in my throat that I have to swallow down. If it is true, and Liam is leaving me and Angela has won, then I'm alone again.

At least for now. At least until Gabby gets back.

chapter 21

There's no way I'm going to talk to Liam right now. I'd rather miss the bus and walk home than see his blue eyes try to pretend that everything is okay.

Because it is not okay.

I am mad. Super mad. I'm zipping my pencil case like it's a wrestling match, throwing my bag, and romper stomping with feet that are itching to kick rocks. Heavy rocks.

I head out towards the other gate, the one where the buses don't pull up. It's on a path past the school office. When I see the door my mouth goes stiff. If no one will tell me where Gabby is, I'll just go and find out myself.

The glass doors are heavy but today I can push them so they fly briskly apart. I enter in a whoosh and let them go behind me. I take in a breath and let it out through my nostrils like steam from a kettle.

"What do you need, dear?" says the woman at the desk. She looks like she's ready to go home for the day. "Did you forget a note or something?"

I walk right up to the counter. "I just want to know how long Gabby is going to be away for," I say firmly.

"Gabby Smeeton. She's in 8D."

"Is she sick?" asks the woman. "There's no way I can know that."

"No," I say. "She got suspended last term. I want to know when she's coming back."

The woman raises her eyebrows and turns to her computer. She taps on the keyboard a few times.

"Smee... what?" she asks, so I spell Gabby's surname out. She looks at the screen and taps a little more.

"That's odd," she says, under her breath, but I can lipread. Her face comes up from the keyboard. "I can't actually tell you anything," she says, and shakes her head slightly.

"Why not?" I ask. "It's not a secret how long other people get suspended for."

"It's not that," she says. And then she just stands there and looks at me, like 'could you go now?' I stare back at her, puzzled. And then I burst into tears. Angry drops of acid that sizzle out of my eyes and burn my cheeks.

Mrs 'I Can't Tell You Anything' narrows her eyes. I can see it through the hot mist around my face. "Are you alright?"

I stamp my foot. "No. I am not alright. I just want to find out where my best friend is and why she won't answer her phone and you say there's nothing you can tell me." The words fly out of my mouth before I can stop them and then I'm deflated, embarrassed and out of energy, all in one hit. I turn to go. "Sorry."

There's a bang and a small rush of air behind me and when I turn, the woman is coming from behind the counter into the office foyer, right up to me. "Do you have to catch a bus?" she asks, looking at her watch.

"No," I sniffle. "I'm going to walk today."

"Come and sit down for a minute," she says, guiding me to an uncomfortable beige, vinyl chair. I allow myself to fall into the seat. Tears are still dropping out of my eyes and, honestly, I can't be bothered to stop them.

The woman sits herself down facing me and leans forward. "Bad day?"

I nod. There's nothing to say.

"Is this Gabby girl your good friend?" she asks.

Again, I nod. "Best friend."

"And she didn't talk to you about anything unusual before the holidays?"

I shake my head. "No."

She sits up straight, takes a deep breath in and twists her face. "Okay. Because of privacy laws I can't actually tell you where Gabby is. But I can tell you this. I can only give out information about students who are enrolled at this school."

I look at her blankly.

"Do you understand me? I can't give you any information about Gabby. I can only give you information about students *who are enrolled here*."

My eyes go big. There's a teeny crack of light into my brain. It slowly gets wider. "You mean she's not…" I look at the woman. "Not enrolled here anymore?"

She repeats it again. "I can only give you infomation about students who are actually *at* this school."

My mouth drops open. Gabby is not at this school any more. Gabby is not enrolled. Gabby has ignored all my messages. Gabby has changed her phone number.

In a flash of light, it all becomes clear. Gabby is not here. She's not coming back.

And I do not have a best friend any more.

"Thanks," I say, and stand up so fast I nearly make myself dizzy. I swallow a few times. "Can I have a drink?" The woman points to a bubbler down the hall and I take shaky steps towards it.

"You okay?" she asks and I nod. But I'm not. And I don't know how long it will be before I am.

The walk home is long but I'm stuck inside my brain, whirling around in my own body. Foot follows hollow foot, hands swing like a robot. I walk past the park with the plum blossom tree and look up to see the pink flowers but they've gone; disappeared into a brown, sludgy mess of rotting petals, smeared all over the grass.

Liam's cheated, Gabby's gone. Liam's cheated, Gabby's gone.

The words are engraved on a hamster wheel in my head and there's a very, very angry hamster running around on it.

A strange car is parked out the front of our house and I look at it for a hard second before I turn my head stiffly towards the front door and march up the steps.

The door is open.

Funny, I think. *Mum's home early*. But then I remember that I've walked and actually, I'm late.

"Mum?" I yell as I stomp down the hall. It's cool and dark but there's sunshine creeping out from under the kitchen door. *At last*, I think. *Food. Drink. Something to make it better.* I throw open the kitchen door, flooding myself with light, my eyes blinking in the brightness, and there, in front of me, is the most extraordinary sight. It's something I've never, ever, seen in this kitchen before.

It's my mum, sitting down, drinking tea with someone else.

A man.

"Mum?"

"Hi, sweetie," says Mum. She sounds normal on the outside but there's a *something* underneath. A something that tells me she's tense.

"Hi," I say. I look at her. And him. His blue shirt, his loosened tie, *his beard*. The way he's arranged his plate in front of him to say *I'm comfortable here;* the way their mugs are nearly touching.

I edge around the walls towards the fridge. "Sandwich," I say. "Homework."

Mum stands up. She smiles, big and wide. Again, normal, but not normal. "Why don't you have a seat. You're hot. I'll get you a drink and make you a sandwich."

"I'm okay," I say, eyes twitching. Now I'm the meerkat. But she insists.

"No, sit down. And say hello to Geoff."

Geoff (at least I presume that Beard Guy is Geoff; there are no other potential Geoffs in the room) lifts his hand in a quick wave-salute thing. "Hey."

His voice is man-deep and it echoes in a way I haven't heard before in this room.

"Hi," I say. I'm wary but I sit. There's not really a choice. "Jazmine," I say.

"Yep. Your mum's told me about you."

I raise my eyebrows and look over at the fridge. Mum has her head down, chopping salad and buttering bread.

Avoiding me. *Funny. She didn't tell me about you,* is what I want to say but I hold it in and tell the angry hamsters to take a tiny break.

"You're in, what, Year 9?" says Geoff. He seems nervous too.

"No. Year 8." I take a deep breath, lift my chin and look at him square in the face.

"Do you drink tea?" he says, gesturing to the pot in front of him.

"Sometimes," I say and I point to his cup. "I usually use that mug."

Mum puts a sandwich down in front of me and comes back to the table. Into the conversation.

"I know Geoff from work," she says brightly. "We've been doing a project together. With some other people."

I look around the table. "So. They didn't come over for tea, then, those other people?"

Mum laughs nervously. "Um, no. They didn't."

"Strange," I say. "That just seems odd. Like, why wouldn't they want to come around too," I can hear myself talking but it doesn't sound like me. It's some other person, taking over my body, opening up doors in my brain to let out words I'd usually store up and hide away.

Mum nods slowly a few times, even though she hasn't said anything and even though there's nothing to agree to. She looks at Geoff who makes a face at her like, 'oh well'.

More doors get opened in my head.

"Did you invite the others?"

Mum looks around her anxiously so I ask it again.

"The other people. Did they get an invite for afternoon tea?"

Now Mum's shutting her eyes like she doesn't want to hear the question. I shift my attention to Geoff. To his credit, he's looking at me full in the face. And to my surprise, he doesn't seem to be angry.

"Geoff," I say. "Did Mum invite everyone else around for afternoon tea?"

He silently shakes his head, three times. *No, no, no.*

I give him a satisfied smile. Maybe even smug. "Okay. Good to know. But still, that seems a bit funny, don't you think?"

Mum opens her eyes. There's a sadness in them.

"That's enough, Jazmine," she says. Shakes her head. "I just wanted you to sit down and have, I don't know, a normal conversation. It's not that hard." She holds her hand to her eye like she's in pain. Geoff looks at her with concern.

I hate seeing Mum like this. I want to help her, to fix her. But my hamsters start running.

"It just seems a bit *unusual*, don't you think," I say, my voice rising, "to make me sit down at a table and talk to a person I've never met and, no offence to you personally, Geoff, you seem to be a nice guy, but you don't seem to be here just as a work team mate."

Geoff shrugs at me and tips his head, like *Fair play, you got me.* I like him, I think. I actually do. But that's not the issue. Not at all. I stand up, tipping my seat back against the cupboards.

"Plus, you haven't actually asked me how my day was." My voice is at yelling pitch. "And if you'd like to know, it was terrible. Really terrible. So to get home and find..." I gesture around the table, "...this (no offence, Geoff)." I burst into tears. "It's just weird." And I run past Geoff and Mum's shocked face straight into my bedroom, slamming the door and throwing myself on the bed.

In my brain, the angry hamsters have done enough. They throw themselves off the wheel and onto their own little beds of straw where they drop into sleep and snore tiny little snickery noises.

I can't sleep. I am pulled apart; hacked into jagged-edged pieces; skin torn off in ugly, bloody strips. My mattress feels like it's cut from rock, bruising and tearing my legs and arms.

On the other side of the door there are low voices; a whispered conversation. Heavy footsteps walk away and a door shuts and then, ten minutes later, Mum taps on my door.

"Can we talk?" she says.

I nod. Shrug. Wipe my eyes. "Whatever."

"I'm sorry," she says. "I wanted that to be so different. I guess I just didn't really know how to do it. It seemed so awkward."

I roll my face towards her.

"Why don't you just say it?" My voice is small, like it's been destroyed. *I would rather just hear it,* I sign.

Mum's face jumps with fear; she clenches her fists into balls, like she's trying hard. "Okay," she says. *Okay. I will.*

She breathes in and then out. I lie and wait, knowing what I'm going to hear, but not wanting to hear it.

"So Geoff is someone I met at work." Her voice is rushing and halting, like she's trying to get it out without saying it wrong. "We've been seeing each other for about two months. I wanted to tell you. I really did. I just didn't know when the best time would be. But I really care about him. I want him to be part of my life." She stops and corrects herself. "Our lives."

Mum knows what I'm going to say. I mean, who wouldn't know? If this was in a book or a movie and I was the main character, of course I'd say it. It's the obvious thing to talk about.

Dad.

But she gets to it before I do.

"I know what you're thinking. And the answer is, no. Of course I'm not forgetting Dad. I could never forget him. It's just, I'm 38. There's still a lot of time left. And Geoff's a good person."

She takes a step towards me, shakes her hands in frustration and blurts it out. "Look. Whatever. Geoff is my boyfriend. I really, really want you to like him. Because I don't want to lose him."

A blurry resignation falls from ceiling to floor, insulating everything. I shut my eyes and look at the red and black swirling patterns behind my eyelids.

"Okay," I say. "Okay," and I nod, slowly. I catch my lips between my teeth and suck them in. "But I can't come out right now. I just can't."

She sits stiffly on my bed. "I'll leave you for a bit then."

She quietly leaves the room, closing the door behind her. I imagine her walking through the kitchen, down the darkened hall to the living room where Geoff opens his arms to hug her and hold her and she sinks into his arms, crying. Crying about me.

I flip myself over and lie on my stomach. Yesterday my life was normal. Great, even. Today, it's been cut down, thrown over, ripped apart.

Every single person I thought was there for me has gone.

I've been abandoned. Again.

chapter 22

Dinner is quiet and awkward, plus I'm not that hungry. Mum has to push me to take a mouthful of peas and the chicken schnitzel tastes like cardboard. I do my homework, water my plants and go to bed before the TV news is finished. Mum's eyes follow me out of the room. I know she wants to talk more but she won't start the conversation and, to be honest, I don't have the energy.

"I love you," she calls after me and I force the words, "You too," out of my throat, but love can't deal with a cheating boyfriend. Love can't get rid of a strange man who's about to take over my mum and change everything about my life. Love can't bring back my best friend.

I put my phone in a drawer (seriously, what's the point of even having it now?) and doodle pointlessly in my journal. The pages are too white and too clean to spoil with the splurging and purging and splashing of blood and tears I want to smear all over them. Colour pens should come with names like 'bitterness', 'anger' and 'rage'. Then we might see some interesting art.

It's not even eight o'clock and my eyes are heavy. I can't be bothered getting into my pyjamas. It's easier just to lie on the bed and stare at the ceiling. I want to sleep, to escape all of this. I want to go back, back to three weeks ago, when things were good, when I had friends.

Back before it all went wrong.

Sleep comes and, with it, a dream. Of course.

This time I'm on a coach, chatting with Gabby next to me and smiling at Liam across the aisle. When I get up to use the bathroom, I can see the usual baddies, driving in a bus behind us. They're going to attack us.

I rush back to my seat. "You guys," I say, in an urgent whisper. "You've got to get off the bus right now," but neither one of them hears me. I pull their faces around with my hand so they are looking right at me. "You've got to get off. They're going to get us." But there's nothing. I'm yelling now, screaming in their faces, stamping my foot on the brightly coloured coach carpet and smashing my fists on the seat. "Do something. Can't you hear me? You've got to get out of here."

But no one is listening. Not Gabby, not Liam, not any of the other passengers in the other seats. It's like talking to myself. Finally I know that I can't save them if they don't want to listen and I throw myself out of the bus, rolling and flipping and hurtling down into the bush on the side of the road.

Yes, I'm safe.

But I'm on my own.

In the morning the only strategy I can come up with for school is to *avoid, avoid, avoid.* I hop off the bus early, walk the rest of the way and go in through the back gate right on nine o'clock. Then I head straight to Science, the first class of the day. There's no Liam and no Angela in this class, so that's good. The teacher, Mr Cox, isn't too bad and the worst I have to deal with is Alvin and the Chipmunks, as I've been affectionately calling them in my head. They're all sitting up at their lab bench already, crowding around a piece of paper in front of them. I pull up a stool. The paper has a bunch of writing on it. I read the heading: *20 jokes that only intellectuals will understand.* Alvin is snorting with laughter and Cammo and Sebastian are giggling like six year olds.

I sit quietly until Alvin turns around. Immediately his face changes and his snorts disappear. He slaps the others over their heads.

"Guys. Stop it. Jazmine's here." They swing around with eyes like saucepans. "Oh. Sorry. Hi." It's a rush of confusion and red cheeks.

"Can I see?" I point to their list of jokes.

"Oh. Sure." Alvin slides it across the table to me. I read it while the chipmunks look on with glee.

"Number five," says Sebastian. "That's the best one."

"No," says Cammo. "It's gotta be eight. Totally eight."

I scan the words but I'm not getting the jokes. Number five seems unintelligible and number eight makes no sense at all.

"Sorry?" I say, screwing up my face in apology. "I mustn't be smart enough."

They rush to reassure me. "Oh, no, it just takes a bit of reading. See, in number five, you've got to look at the meaning of Newton..." But Alvin cuts them off with his hand. "Hey, if it's not her thing, that's cool," he says. He turns to me. "You're smart. Don't worry about it." He pulls his lab stool over next to me, comfortable for once.

"So. Are you free to work on the project this week? What about in the library at lunch today?"

I nod and smile. It's a relief. "Sure."

At recess I go to the canteen for a sandwich and then the bathroom on the other side of the school campus. I manage to avoid Liam for the entire morning and then spend lunch in the library talking about leaves, autumn colours, the very best way to set up a testing protocol and how to use a spreadsheet to display the results.

Alvin's passion for his subject is amusing at first. I can't quite believe that someone is going to put this much effort into a science project, but then, somehow, his enthusiasm rubs off and I get keen myself. I surprise myself by discovering that I've got opinions about bar graphs versus pie charts and, even more surprisingly, that I'm going to let everyone know what they are, even *if* Cammo has a different idea.

"No Jazmine," he says, almost banging the table in frustration. "Pie charts aren't as easy to read. They just aren't."

"But I think they look great," I say. "Everyone does bar graphs. All the time. It's kind of standard."

"Standard for a reason," he says.

"Yeah, but do you want to be standard?" I ask. My eyes are flashing with enjoyment. I've never been in an argument like this before and I like it. "You don't want to be like everyone else. The project will be the best, so make it look awesome too."

Cammo puts his hand down and tilts his head. "Maybe you're right," he says, like he's never thought of it that way before. To my left, Alvin beams a huge smile and Sebastian digs him in the shoulder. I pretend not to see it.

We're out of the library when the bell goes and my next class is English. I've almost forgotten my worries but as I approach the classroom they all come flooding back. Liam's waiting for me.

My smile disappears and I can feel my back stiffen up and my face go tense. Liam, on the other hand, is all sunshine and goodness.

"Jaz!" he says, bouncing up to me. I hardly know where to look. "Where have you been all day? I thought you must be sick or something and you didn't answer my texts."

"Phone's at home," I mutter but he hardly seems to notice.

"I'm missing you," he says, and he gives me a pouty look. I think it's supposed to be funny but it's hard to laugh. It's hard to say anything, actually. I look away and keep walking but he doesn't take the hint.

"I'll sit with you, okay?" he says and plonks himself down at the desk next to mine, so close that our elbows and knees are touching. I try to pull away but there's nowhere else to go except off the other side of the chair and the teacher wouldn't be very happy about that so I have to stay there, squashed up next to Liam, uncomfortable and mad.

The teacher starts talking about Shakespeare. I'm trying to listen but Liam wants to pass me notes.

Walk home with me today? I've got something to show you.

I take it and look at it. Then I shrug and shake my

head but he frowns.

Why not? You okay? You're either sick or you're avoiding me... He draws a smiley face underneath and looks across at me with his blue eyes.

Call me crazy, but I still swoon. A little bit of my heart decides that *surely, a walk can't be that bad,* and *maybe it's not true, all of it with Angela,* and *maybe I've just misunderstood something. After all, I did go off and leave him for the holidays...*

And he grins at me. He knows he's got me. I know he's got me. I know he knows he's got me. And part of me is not sorry. Not one little bit. *Avoid, avoid, avoid.* The plan works, until he looks you in the eyes and whirls his lasso of gorgeousness.

We walk home together, side by side, our hands brushing each other occasionally, but nothing else. He asks me about my holidays. I tell him small things at first; we went out to eat, I went on a boat, it was fun. Then I tell him the bigger things; the storm, Grandma's ankle and wrist, running down the mountain to get help and back up again. By the time we get outside my place I'm at the part of trying to call the ambulance and sitting in the rain, waiting.

"You must have been so scared," he says. His voice sounds strong and sympathetic. "You must have been just crying with the worry."

"Yes," I say, immediately. "Really scared. But that was only at the beginning. By the end I was fine and..."
But he doesn't seem to hear me. Instead, he turns to me, his hand on my wrist, like he wants to stop me from walking. His eyes find mine and he looks deep and long

at me.

"I would never put you in that kind of position. Where you had to rescue me. If I'd been there, I would have done it for you." He reaches out for my other hand and shakes his head slowly. "Poor you. Really. Poor you."

I feel uncomfortable and look around me. Mum's car isn't there. There are a few cars in the street, but I don't recognise any of them. "It wasn't really like that," I say, but he doesn't listen. Instead, he comes in closer and his voice gets quieter.

"Jazmine, all I could think about was you, all holidays. But you weren't here. I nearly went crazy, missing you." He reaches in to my face but I duck away and pull one wrist free.

"You didn't text me much," I say. My voice is wobbly.

"I couldn't," he says. "It was too hard. You weren't here. Texting isn't the same. Even talking on the phone isn't the same. I couldn't stand it. You can't go away again, okay?"

Now I feel weird. Really weird.

"I might go away. In fact, I probably will. I really liked visiting my grandma."

He tries to grab my other wrist but this time I don't let him get halfway.

"I've got to go, Liam," I say and pull away from him. "You've got to go. Your mum will wonder where you are."

"Is that it?" he says. His voice is angry now. "Is that all I get? After you avoid me all holidays, and for ages before that too?"

I shrug. "I don't know what you want," I say, pulling

out my keys from my bag. "I'm sorry."

"You do know," he says. He steps forward, once, twice, three times. I'm scared, backing up to the front door. "You do know and you just play with me. You're a tease."

He grabs my hand and I don't know what to do, how to shake him off, how to make him go away. I've got the house keys in my free hand but I can't reach the door, and even if I did open it, would he decide to come in after me?

But then there's the slam of a car door and heavy footsteps and Liam steps back, all on his own, like he's falling back into his shell or retreating underground, and there's a voice that surrounds me, like a cloud of rescue; a big, bearded voice that says, "Jazmine. Do you know if your mum's home yet?"

chapter 23

On Thursday and Friday I do something I've never done before in my entire life.

I refuse to go to school.

"Are you sick?" Mum asks, the first day, sitting on the side of my bed where I've stayed, in my pyjamas, since six o'clock, an hour and a half ago.

"No."

"Have you got a headache?"

"No. I said I wasn't sick."

"Are you worried about something?" she asks.

I look away to the wall.

"I just don't want to."

She gives me more time but I don't move and fifteen minutes later she's back.

"You'll miss the bus unless you get going."

"I know," I say.

"I've got to go to work. If you hurry I could drop you off, just for today."

"It's not the bus," I say.

She flings up her hands. Annoyance? Resignation? I can't tell.

"I can't make you get out of bed Jazmine," she says.

"But unless you move, you're going to make yourself, and me. late."

I stare at the wall.

"Is it one of your friends? Is someone bullying you again? I can call the school and we can sort it out, you know. Tell the deputy principal? Surely Liam would look after you, wouldn't he?"

Under my blankets my heart starts up again. I can feel a flush rising in my cheeks so I shrug my doona up past my neck but I'm safe. Mum doesn't know about yesterday afternoon.

"Jazmine, is your mum home yet?" Geoff had asked from nowhere and I'd turned to see his beard and his bulk taking up the path where Liam had stood just seconds before. My head turned again, in the opposite direction, to see Liam halfway down the street. *Running, even?*

I stammered a reply, voice shaky and hands wobbling. "Not sure. No. Don't think so," and held up my key to show him I'd only just gotten back myself.

"She asked me to stop by. I've been working at the other office," he said, explaining himself.

"Oh," I said, trying to control my chest. It wanted to collapse into sobs. My eyes were having trouble focusing and I needed to blink away tears.

"Someone you know?" Geoff nodded towards Liam, getting smaller and smaller in the distance.

My chin went up and down of its own accord. "It's Liam."

His brows furrowed. "The boyfriend?" And then he looked slightly guilty, like he was trying to apologise.

"Sorry. Just, your mum told me about him."

I let a half-smile escape. "Yep," I said, "the boyfriend."

His face went serious again. "Maybe you need to rethink that."

I opened my eyes wide and gave him a look like, 'who are you to say something like that?' and he flipped his palms up towards me. "Hey, I'm sorry. Not my business." He looked around him a few times. "Okay. So, I'll push off. Tell your mum I called by?"

I nodded and watched him walk back to his car, get in and drive away. He tooted the horn as he drove off and for some reason it made me smile. I put my hand up in one of those 'see ya' waves people do and kept it up until I saw his car disappear around the corner.

"Thanks," I said quietly. Just so I could hear it myself. And then I turned and let myself into the house.

Later, I told Mum that Geoff had been here.

"Did he say something?" she said.

"Yeah. Just, 'Tell your mum I called by'."

"That's it?"

"That's it."

Something crossed her face and then she shook her hair, smiled and said, "Thanks so much for talking to him."

I shrugged. "Whatever."

I said nothing about Liam. I said nothing about Geoff's voice plucking me out of a stormy sea. I said nothing about Angela or the party and the stories about the kissing, or the worry that maybe I was the one to blame for it all. I said nothing about the fact that I felt like I was on one of those terrible, dizzy, spinning fairground rides whenever I spent time with Liam, the person who was supposed to like me more than anyone.

Mum didn't know any of it.

And I wasn't about to tell her. Every time I thought about it, my stomach turned into a crater of swirling embarrassment. I felt tiny and terrified. And full of dread. Before, I just would have turned invisible; refused to feel any of it. But that doesn't work anymore. So I'll do the next best thing; just not turn up.

Bed is my only option.

"You have to go." Mum's trying one last time, in a pleading voice, to get me up and out, but it's not going to work.

"I'm not going."

I curl myself towards the wall tighter and listen for the door to close as Mum leaves.

On Friday she runs through a whole range of strategies. There's the comforting, 'poor Jazmine' tactic ('oh sweetie, I know you don't want to, but I can give you a lift'), the straight talking, tough love ('young lady, you're going to have to do this and suck it up, whether you like it or not'), the panicky, I-don't-want-people-to-think-I'm-a-bad-mother desperation ('Please? Please get out of bed. I'm going to have to ring the school if you don't…').

But I don't get out of bed. I can't.

It's just too hard.

Mum goes to work. I can see the worry on her face as she fusses around the kitchen, packing her lunch and washing the breakfast dishes, but I can't make it better. I can't make my own worries better. How could I possibly deal with hers too?

I spend the day sleeping, watering the garden, drawing in my journal. Oh, and ignoring my phone which keeps beeping in my drawer until I take out my hearing aid so that I can't hear it any more. *Liam, maybe?* I don't know, and I don't want to find out. After lunch I pull out the science project sheets and do some work on the bit I'm supposed to be doing. The time disappears and I'm genuinely surprised at how quickly the times goes by until Mum gets home, her mouth straight, her steps solid and her eyes set.

"Hey," I say, putting my hearing aid back in.

She takes in a quick breath and puts on a firm smile.

"Hi Jazmine. I need you to come with me in the car, okay?"

"Pyjamas," I say, gesturing down at my pink monkeys and cartoon palm trees.

"Doesn't matter," she says. "PJs are fine."

I consider it for a few seconds. School's finished so we can't be going there. She doesn't know where Liam lives, so she can't take me to him. Maybe it's just the shops and I can sit in the car park while she goes in. I squint my eyes, weighing it up. I think I might be safe.

"Okay," I say. "Now?"

"Mmm-hmm," she says. "Just pop in the car and I'll be there in a minute."

I head outside. It's sunny with a wide, perfect sky; the sort of day that would have made me happy a few weeks ago. Now, though, it just mocks. Laughs at me. I get in the front seat of the car and screw up my face at the blueness above, daring it to leave and send in clouds instead.

Mum takes a few minutes and when she finally locks the front door and comes around to her side I notice she's got a bag with her. She slips it into the back and then buckles herself in.

"Let's go," she says, throwing a bottle of water at me.

I take a sip. "Where to?"

"You'll see."

We drive past the turnoff to the main street, past the supermarket and right out past the edge of town where the hardware barn is. I look over at her with a question on my face but she's not looking at me. She's focusing, hard, on the road.

"So, out of town?" I say.

She nods.

"Longish drive?" I ask.

She nods again.

"Have I been there before?"

She looks over at me with an exasperated face. "Figure it out, Jazmine."

I sit and think. There's really only one option. But it seems nuts.

"Grandma's?"

Mum nods.

"You're taking me to Grandma's on a Friday night in my pyjamas?"

She sighs. "Desperate measures," and shakes her head. She waits for a second and then starts talking again. Pouring it out onto my lap. "I mean, really. What did you think I was going to do? Let you stay home from school for the rest of your life? I hardly know how to handle this new 'I'll do what I want' thing from you. If you won't tell me what's going on, maybe you'll tell your Grandma. Maybe she can help you sort it out."

I feel squashed into my seat; pushed back by an invisible force. We drive and drive and two and a half hours later I've drunk all the water and we're winding up the hill towards Grandma's place, heading for her twinkling lights.

"This is really embarrassing," I say. "How can I even get out of the car?"

Mum grimaces. "We've all been embarrassed. Get used to it."

When we pull into Grandma's driveway and I feel the grumble of gravel under the wheels I shut my eyes and sink into the seat covers but then the door opens and there's Grandma's face in mine, smiling like she's pleased to see me.

I can get out of the car.

Mum has a quick conversation with Grandma and then an even quicker one with me.

"Okay, I'm coming back for you Sunday. Your stuff's in the bag."

"Oh."

She pecks me on the cheek, hops back in her seat and drives off into the black. We watch her headlights twist and turn as she winds back down the mountain road.

"This is nice," says Grandma, when the lights finally become pinpricks in a straight line of other tiny ant cars. She puts her good arm around me. "It's great to see you."

"Yeah. In my pyjamas." My head drops, embarrassed. Grandma takes a good look. "I think they're cute," she says. "Monkeys. Better than boring old stripes."

I laugh. "I threw out my striped pair a few months ago."

"Well you picked good ones," she says and we go inside. The lamps make it look cozy and warm. "Sit down and I'll get you some dinner."

"Are you better?" I ask. "How's the arm?"

"Improving all the time," she says. "I can even cook now. One-handed, but still…"

She brings me an omelette with mushrooms and cheese that squeaks in my teeth.

"What is this stuff?" I ask. "It's weird."

"Haloumi," she says, with a wide grin. "Do you love it?"

I grin back. "Love it."

Later, she puts me to bed, back in my old room.

"I'd offer to read you a story but you're probably too old for that," she says, sitting on the edge of the mattress.

"Maybe a bit," I say. I look around the room and then at Grandma. The room is warm and the bed is comfortable but I feel tight inside. "Did Mum tell you why she brought me?"

"A little," she says. She touches my face and smoothes my hair. "Why don't you just get some sleep for now. We can talk about what needs to be talked about in the morning."

My stomach relaxes. I nod. "Okay." But then a new fear pushes its way up into my throat. "Sometimes I have trouble sleeping though."

Grandma raises her eyebrows. "Really? Why's that?"

I open my mouth but no words come. I've never told anyone about the men with machine guns, the spirits with leather faces, the rocket attacks, the ceaseless runnings through the night. I've never told anyone about the things that want to kill me, that look for me and find me no matter how good I think my hiding place is, that keep searching and keep chasing even when I'm begging them to stop, to please, please, just go away.

I swallow.

"Dreams."

Grandma tips her head to one side. "A lot?"

I nod.

"Most nights?"

I nod again.

She frowns slightly.

"They feel real," she says. "They feel so real. But you know what? They're not. And in a dream you can choose the ending."

chapter 24

I have dreams. Of course I do. They, the whoever-they-are, the terrible-horribles of the night, chase me while I run and run, puffing and aching, heart thumping out of my chest and legs crying out for mercy. They threaten me with knives and fists and slingshots. They yell terrible insults.

I know I have to get away. I just don't know how.

And then, for the first time ever, something changes.

Hiding, breathing fast, behind a rock in the forest, I know, really know, that I am in a dream.

I'm asleep. The thought is as refreshing as the first sip of a cold drink on a sweltering day.

And then something else.

I can choose the ending.

I lean quietly around the rock and peer out. They're still coming for me. Can I think them away? Magically will them to steer off in the other direction? I clench my dream hands and think my dream thoughts but the baddies are still coming. *Try harder,* I say to myself. *Choose again.* My fingernails rip into my skin, I'm clenching everything so much, my teeth are grinding themselves down. But it doesn't work. There's a yell and a shriek and evil wolves are on me, nipping and tearing at my hair. I'm melting with fear and pounding with terror and then I wake up. Alone in my bed.

Safe. But very, very scared.

Choose the ending? I don't think so.

I can't shut my eyes again so I lie still and look out the window at the garden. The creeping dawn light is stretching its fingers across the grass, turning black to grey and grey to a pale version of whatever the colours would be in the sunlight. Grandma has had a tree taken out since last week. She was talking about it before; how the roots were disturbing the foundations of the house and stealing water from the other plants. I felt sorry for it, begged her not to get rid of it, but it's gone now. And the hole is raw and gaping.

"It's the other plants you should feel sorry for," she said. "They're the ones that can't live their lives. Some trees think they can take over everything else. And in my garden, they go."

The light gets brighter and I can see movement outside. Grandma's up early, despite her sprained ankle, hobbling around on a big foot support thing that looks like a massive black boot. She's carrying a plant in a small pot in her good hand and is heading towards the hole.

I've been in my PJs for two days so I figure a third won't hurt and I pad down the hall and out the back door. Grandma's on her knees, digging and sorting the soil around the hole where the tree was.

"Are you going to plant something else there?" I ask.

She turns to see me, surprise on her face. "Good

morning. It's early. Are you sure you want to get up?"

I kneel beside her. "Want some help?"

She beams. "It's another plum blossom tree. I had the camphor laurel taken out. Time to replant."

"It's pretty," I say, and start to dig with my hands. The cool dirt feels rich under my fingertips. We work together, digging, planting, watering and mulching, me looking out for Grandma's wrist and ankle, and she protesting, but always with a smile, that I'm doing too much.

When it's done and we're done and the hose is turned off, the tools put away and our fingernails scrubbed to get most of the dirt out, we have breakfast out on the deck. Eggs, orange juice, toast and jam. I'm hungry again after three days of taking only enough bites of anything to keep Mum off my back.

"I tried to choose the ending of my dream," I say, mouth full of toast. "It didn't work."

Grandma sips her tea. "Sometimes, depending on the dream, it's enough just to choose." She looks out across the escarpment. "Sometimes, though, you have to fight."

I think about it, but a shudder goes through me.

"I couldn't," I say. "I wouldn't know how to even start. And what if they won?" The toast goes to cardboard in my mouth.

"If you don't try, they've won anyway," Grandma says. She throws a scrap of crust out onto the lawn. A small red and brown bird swoops down to pick it up. "The more you run and hide, the more they'll chase you."

I look up accusingly. "How did you know?"

"What?"

"My dreams. The running and hiding bit."

Grandma laughs. "Really? Oh, my darling Jazmine. You're certainly not the first to have those dreams. And you won't be the last."

I'm silent for a minute.

"I didn't know," I say. "I didn't know that other people have the same thing."

Grandma butters a piece of bread and puts her knife down.

"Everybody has the same everything," she says. "If you can find one problem or one fear or one dread or, even, one happiness that no one else has ever had, it's only because you haven't talked to enough people."

As I sit, looking at the view, it seems to get bigger. Wider. Wilder. It's like I can see further out of my eyes.

"Grandma, I need to ask you."

She looks up, mouth full of bread. I laugh because she looks so funny and she giggles too.

"Sorry." She wipes her chin where a tiny bit of jam has found its way down.

"That poster thing in my room. What does it mean, 'that is not what ships are built for?'"

Her eyes get bright. "I *love* that, don't you? I saw it once when I was on holidays in Queensland. I bought it straight away and posted it home."

I nod. "It's nice. I like the boat. It reminds me of Adrian's one. But I'm just not sure if I get it."

She thinks for a moment. "I guess it's like, you know, there are so many ways people try to be safe, to protect themselves in life."

"Like staying home a lot?"

"That's one. There are more. Maybe, always doing the same thing. Drinking too much. Never wanting to learn. Not being able to say sorry. Sometimes we build these harbours for ourselves so we'll be protected. So we won't ever have to feel bad. Or face bad people."

"But isn't that normal?" I ask. "I don't want to feel bad."

Grandma tips her head to the side. "No one does. But it's part of life. And if you don't ever feel bad, you can never feel glorious either." She picks up her fork and twirls it around, like she's conducting an orchestra. "A small life is staying in the harbour you build for yourself. You're protected, but you don't get the amazing things life has to offer. A big life, out on the ocean, in the fast winds and on the big waves is riskier and scarier, but it's so much better. I mean, who doesn't like tropical islands and beaches and bays? You don't see those if you stay in your harbour."

She takes a breath. "And, like it says, it's what we're built for."

"Facing bad people is what I'm built for?" I say.

"Well, that, and also finding great people," Grandma laughs. "Life's not all terrible heartbreak, you know. There's a lot of that, but it's not all there is."

"Sometimes it seems like it." I think, but I don't say it.

We work in the garden for the rest of the morning and after lunch Grandma announces that she needs to get some groceries.

"Adrian will pick us up at two," she says. "Do you have anything you want to get from the shops?"

The mall is still busy at half past two, even though

everything shuts at four. Saturdays at the shops are obviously pretty popular here, judging from the groups of teenagers hanging out. The shops are the usual collection of small town stores; a few chains, a few independents and a couple of discount outlets. I browse while Grandma and Adrian get the groceries; dawdle through a jewellery store, a surf shop and then a bookshop. I'm in the cooking section looking at recipe books when a group of five girls, all about my age, head for the fiction shelves at the back.

And then I hear something that makes my hair go static and my body prickle up.

It's the sound of a voice I haven't heard for a long time.

It's loud, constant and cheerful.

It's the voice of someone I know.

Gabby.

Gabby?

That can't be right, I think to myself. I put my finger into the cookbook I'm looking at, close it and poke my head around the shelf.

I can't really see who's there. The other girls, who are clearly *not* Gabby, are blocking my view and there's a mum with two toddlers in the way as well. I go back to my recipes, shaking my head, my eyes glancing over a section called `10 Ways to use Quinoa'. Maybe I should get this for Grandma for Christmas, I think to myself. She'd love it. But then I hear it again.

"No seriously, you guys. You *have* to get this book. It's the best book ever. It's like the king of all books. I was obsessed with it for weeks. I'm still obsessed."

It's her voice.

Those are her words.

It must be her.

I step out, push past the toddlers and through the group of girls. There in front of me is my best friend, Gabby. The person who stood up for me, protected me and got suspended for me. My eyes are saucers and I can hardly move. But my face is smiling like I've just been given a puppy.

"Gab!" I say, and I move in for a hug.

In slow motion, I see Gabby's face flit from surprise to recognition to terror. And then it changes one more time. To a blank nothing. She sidesteps the hug and leaves me hurtling towards a shelf of books about vampires. I bang my chin on the edge.

Ouch.

I whirl around, confused. Am I dreaming? Is it just someone who looks like her? I stare again, but I'm not wrong. It's definitely Gabby. Her build, her hair, her style of clothes. She's even wearing rainbow toe socks on her feet. I can see the toes through her open shoes.

"Gabby?" I say, but this time it's a question, and there's disbelief on my face.

She looks at me, through me and past me. And then she says to her friends, in her voice that I know means 'I've had enough now. I'm upset'; she says, "Let's go, you guys."

There's a whisk and whoosh of air and then Gabby and her friends (new friends?) are gone, out of the shop, heading back into the mall.

I rub my chin. No blood. But there will be a bruise.

I'm shocked and confused and whirling and going crazy. Is it really her? If it is, what have I done to make her behave this way? And then, in one long, quick, furious rush of red, I am angry.

Sometimes you have to fight.

Now is the time.

I move out of the bookshop fast, hitting a pile of thriller novels as I go. "Sorry," I say, but I don't stop to pick them up. I need to get to Gabby. My shoes slide on the shiny mall tiles but I run anyway.

"Gabby," I say when I've caught up to her. I say it loudly, with her voice, so that everyone will listen.

"Gabby. You have to listen to me."

Her friends turn around to see me, a strange girl; red-faced and breathless, yelling at them, demanding attention, but Gabby stays faced in her one direction, turned away from me, her back to my face.

"Is that Gabby?" I ask her friend, black haired and blue eyed, wearing jeans and a yellow t-shirt. "Is that Gabby Smeeton?"

She frowns at me, confused. "Yeah."

"Does she live here?"

The girl looks confused. "Not here. But in Mollymook."

"Make her turn around," I say. Demanding, firm, fighting. "Make her talk to me."

She taps Gabby on the shoulder. "This girl says she knows you," she says, her voice going up at the end. Like a question.

Gabby shakes her head and her friend shrugs her shoulders at me. "She doesn't want to. You should maybe go."

The red surges into my face. "I will not go," I say. "I will stay and I will talk to her. Even if she won't talk to me." I walk around the group so I can see Gabby's face. She lowers her eyes to the floor. My heart is beating crazy-furious but I have to say the words that are rushing into my mouth.

"Why didn't you phone me? Why did you cut me off? I can't understand it. I've been so worried, and so upset. Did you get suspended? What even happened? I'm so mad, and now you're acting like, I don't know, like you don't even know who I am. I'm your best friend, aren't I? You even said so. Maybe I haven't been a good best friend, I don't know. But I tried, didn't I? And I miss you."

My words come out in a big gush and then trail off into nothing. I look at her one more time, but she still won't face me and I know there's nothing I can do. I walk away and sit on a bench like an old person, resting my head in my hands. Gabby's friends regroup, their shocked mouths going double time. *Did you hear that? What was she on about? Oh my gosh, I can't believe it…* They move away, chattering and looking back with looks of, first, hatred, then pity, then just plain 'she's nuts'.

And all I can do is sit and wait.

chapter 25

When Grandma and Adrian emerge from the supermarket which is all brightly lit with glossy, smiling, fruit-eating images, I can't hold back the tears. A dam door has been pulled up and a lake's worth of crying is falling out.

"Jazmine," says Grandma. "You okay?" She looks concerned, as far as I can see through wet, steamed up eyes and she pulls my shoulders towards her so she can see my face.

"Did something happen?" she asks, but I can't answer. All I can do is look in the direction Gabby and her friends went and gabble something about 'over there, and then she wouldn't look at me and cut me off and…'

"Take a breath," she says, so I push my chest out and in a few times. "Can you stop crying?"

I gulp a few sobs down and do that sniffy, breathless thing. "I think so."

"Let's go to a café." It's Grandma's answer for everything. She grasps my hand tightly and I'm too miserable to be embarrassed about it in public. Plus it feels good. Strong. Like I'm not alone.

The café is dark brown with dim lights and comfy seats.

There's no music playing and hardly any customers so it's easy to hear every word Grandma says. I put myself into the chair and rub my eyes. "Sorry," I say. "I'm really sorry."

Adrian leans over and pats my hand. Kind of like a grandpa would do, I guess. "Don't apologise," he says. His smile is like the radiator heater Mum puts on at home when it starts getting cold at night, before she decides she can afford to switch on the real heating. Just being close to it makes me feel snug.

We order coffee. That is to say, Grandma orders some kind of hazelnut thing, Adrian gets a pot of tea and I get talked into a hot chocolate. "It'll help," says Grandma, after I've shaken my head a bit.

"And we'll have that pistachio and cranberry toast of yours as well," she says to the waitress. "Lots of it."

Then she turns to me. "Now. Do you think you can talk about it?"

I start, restart and correct myself some more before it all finally comes out. "And she just wouldn't even look at me."

"You're sure it was her?" Adrian says.

"It was her. But it was like she was pretending she didn't know who I was."

The coffees and fruit loaf slices arrive and for half a minute we play jigsaw puzzles on the table trying to find a way to fit it all on. I sip my drink. Grandma was right. It does help.

"So the real question is, what do you want to do about this?" asks Grandma, squelching melted butter in her mouth. Adrian hands her a napkin.

My brain is stuck. "What do you mean?"

"What do you want to do about this?" Grandma says. "What do you want to happen?"

In my head, somewhere, a cymbal goes off. *Boonnnngggg*. A big, clangy, echoey sound; a sound I've never heard before. My eyes open wide. Grandma's words have grown arms, reached out and shaken me. I've never seen things this way before and it is so stunningly clear and easy that I can't believe it's taken me until the age of 14 to get it.

"I have a choice," I say. Slowly, to myself.

Grandma thinks I'm talking to her so she answers me. "Yes. You do."

A seedling of courage sprouts and grows in my chest and I know what I'm going to do.

"I want to find her. I want to look for Gabby."

Back at Grandma's, with groceries put away and extra cups of tea made and drunk, Adrian sets me up on the computer.

"I know a bit about it," he says, fussing around the mouse. "But you're probably all up to date with how the google thing and the wiki-whatsits and everything work."

I smile and nod and say thank you but when it's just me facing a blank screen, I realise I have no idea how to find someone who's disappeared. Gabby's not on Facebook or anything. She always said she wasn't interested in 'being stalked', as she put it.

Erin argued with her. "It's not stalking. It's just saying hi to your friends."

"Are you my friend?" Gabby asked her.

"Duh."

"So, hi."

It's pointless to look on social media so I try to remember the company Gabby said her dad worked for and search for a list of their staff but it's too big and the website is just about how amazing their vision for the future is, all in really, really long words, so I get into a dead end. I google her mum but she doesn't have a blog or anything so then I'm stuck and about to feel like *this was all a stupid idea* and that *I'm doomed to fail* and *why even try, rah rah rah...*

And then it hits me.

The obvious solution.

I put Gabby's surname into the White Pages, take a tiny breath and hit enter. Up come four listings for the South Coast. And one of them is in Mollymook.

"There's a phone number," I say. Grandma hands me the phone and I take it and ring the number, hardly daring to breathe while I do. The phone purrs a few times and then someone picks it up and says 'Hello?' and it's Gabby's mum, friendly and happy and familiar.

"Hey, is that Mrs Smeeton?" I say. My stomach is in pieces but I'm going to keep going anyway. "It's Jazmine here. From before. I used to hang out with Gabby."

I don't know what I'm expecting but it's certainly not a happy, delighted voice on the other end of the phone, asking me how I am.

"It's been ages," she says. "How's school going?"

"Good," I say. I'm still kind of scared but I take a deep breath and almost shout it out. "I'm visiting my Grandma and she lives close. Can I come over and see Gab?"

Adrian is a kind man, I think to myself, as he drives us all the 45 minutes to Mollymook, but now's probably not the time to ask Grandma if they're going to get married. She's sitting in the front, looking out the window and pointing out things as they fly past.

"That's the harbour," she says, nodding at the blue and gold speckled water across the other side of the road. "You can get down to the breakwater that way."

"Can we go there?" I say suddenly. "Can we stop there on the way?"

"We're really close to Gabby's place," says Adrian. "Are you sure?"

"Sure I'm sure," I say. I'm gripped with an urgent need to breathe. To clear my head. To get brave.

Adrian makes a swing to the right and we head down the tree-lined street towards the beach. There's a jutting peninsula of rock and random, piled-up concrete megablocks ahead of us, with a path out to the horizon.

Grandma is slow on her ankle; Adrian helps her with her crutch, and I run ahead into the breeze and the salt and the tiny drops of spray. On the ocean side the waves break on the rocks, foaming and crashing and smashing apart but on the harbour side the water is still and calm, reflecting the sunlight back at me like a golden mirror. *Out there. In here.* I want to look at the boats and the buoys and the tiny ripples of life in the flat water but my eyes keep getting drawn beyond the rocks, right out to the never-ending straight line of *what's beyond*.

I walk to the absolute end of the breakwater and then climb out onto the boulders as far as I can go without giving Grandma a heart attack. The wind is flapping my hair and bawling in my ears and looking out, I feel like I'm completely alone. But for once, it doesn't matter. There is the harbour, and there is out there, the rest of life. And I know which way I want to go.

I throw my hands up and out and inhale everything, all of the things, all the air and spray and life and colour and then I breathe it all out again, all at once.

Time to fight.

Gabby's new place is almost identical to where she lived before. New street, new house, new driveway, new garden. Everything's shiny as well. And kind of the same as everything else around it.

"Do you want to go in on your own?" asks Grandma.

"Probably," I say. "Will you wait?"

"As long as it takes."

I get out of the car. The driveway seems long, but maybe that's just my nerves. They've got the same doorbell as before. I ring it. There's a click and a bang and the door opens and there, before me, mouth wide open in disbelief, is Gabby.

"Hey," I say, and I watch her face. No change. Just pure stunned mullet. Then she shakes herself alive again and goes to close the door. I've thought this out, though. I'm prepared. I'm just about to stick my foot in the door like they do in the movies, even though I think it will probably hurt with sandals on. Thankfully, I get to keep my feet intact. Out through the hallway, into the light comes Gabby's mum.

"Jazmine!" she says, her face lit up with a smile. "So glad you came by! Gabby, I forgot to tell you when you got home. Jazmine called and said she was nearby so I said *of course* you'd love to see her."

I raise my eyebrows at her and step inside as Gabby's mum sweeps open the door. Gabby's face is a mixture of pain and fury but I look past it. This is about getting answers, that's all. We stand awkwardly in the entrance for a few seconds until her mum rescues the situation. "Well, don't just look at each other, girls. Come on in, Jaz. Are you hungry? I've got home made mini quiches."

We eat (quiche and cookies) and drink (home made lemon and ginger squash) and I carry on some kind of stilted conversation with Mrs-Smeeton-I-mean-Ann while Gabby sulks over her drink and then it's really time. To talk.

"Gab, are you going to take Jazmine upstairs? Show her your room?" says her mum. She points to the staircase and makes meaningful nodding faces. Gabby lets out a stifled groan and drags herself off her chair.

I keep my face calm and follow her up the stairs (shiny brown timber with a stainless steel railing) and through a freshly painted white door. She shuts the door behind me and leans back against it, face turned away and hands behind her back.

"What?" she says. Her voice is tired. "What do you even want?"

chapter 26

There's a silence hanging between us. Gabby still won't look at me. She just stands there, face turned away, her foot jiggling.

I don't talk. Instead I look around her room. It's a different shape to the old room. Bigger and more of a square. But everything's come with her; the boy band posters, the crammed bookshelves and her laptop on her white computer desk. The big double bed seems smaller in here but it's still stuffed with cushions and soft toys. And then I spy a familiar ear poking out of a crowd of fur.

"Wally?"

My face breaks into a smile and I climb on the bed and pull Gabby's wombat out of the pile. He's still wearing the ribbon Gabby put on him to bring him to school. I hug him close and snuggle his nose to mine.

"So cute!" I say, and then I sit on the bed, looking at Gabby, waiting for her to smile as well.

She doesn't.

Instead she scuffs her toe against the carpet.

"You should just go, Jaz," she says. Her voice is heavy.

My eyebrows furrow. "I just wanted to see how you are. Where you went."

She plays with the tie from her dressing gown, hanging from a hook on the door. "Why would you even care?"

I can feel my face start to go red. "Because you're my friend? Because, maybe, I miss you?"

"You don't even know me," she says. "So you can't actually miss 'me'. Like, logic?"

"I do know you." I sputter the words. "You're my best friend."

"You think I am. You want me to be. But I'm not really that person." She turns her face to look at me. Her eyes are hard. And sad.

I swallow; hold Wally a little tighter.

"I have no idea what you're talking about." I can hear a waver in my voice. "You're not making any sense."

Gabby sighs, a long, hard, tired breath out. She slides down the door onto the floor, pulling her dressing gown with her.

"Look. Jazmine. I'll say this once, okay? And then you'll understand it. And then you can go." She breathes in and out again and looks up to the ceiling. "We move. That's what we do. My dad's job makes him move, like, every year or two. So I change schools. And, every time, I find people I can hang out with, and I'm happy and I'm funny and I find some people who like me, and it's okay." She puts her head down and digs her finger into the carpet. "But it's not me. That's what no one gets. It's not really me. The Gabby you think you know isn't the real one. So when I leave, you don't miss me, because I was never really there, and, because it wasn't really me, I never really cared about any of you."

She looks straight at me. "Do you get that?"

I can hear her words echoing around in my head but I'm not processing them. There's something wrong with what she's saying. I just can't figure out what it is. I look over at her closet, clothes falling out of it as usual; the pile of books standing scruffily next to her bed; her shoes dashed off and left around the room.

And then I know what's wrong.

She's wrong.

I smile at her. Broadly. She's not expecting it and I can see surprise in her eyes.

I shrug, happily.

"You're wrong."

She flinches. "What?"

"I said you're wrong." I throw my arm around the room. "Look. Nothing's changed. You're still a messy slob. You still leave your stuff around. You still like *them.*" I gesture to the smiling boys on the wall, hair all flicked and collars up like they're trying to impress.

Gabby follows my hand. "So?"

"So, I'm saying, your room's still the same. You're the same." I put Wally down next to me. "And you're lying about not caring about any of us."

She pouts and her face looks angry but it's more of an embarrassed anger than anything.

"You stood up for me at school when you could have just ignored me. You hung out with me after school when you didn't have to. You gave me your mum's cupcakes and stuff to eat. Plus you did something totally nuts that just proves it."

Gabby chews on her mouth and narrows her eyes. "What?"

"You got suspended for me, doofus. You stormed right up to Angela and slapped her on the face. I saw it. You can't pretend you didn't." I'm laughing as I say it. "I'm sorry, Gab. I just don't buy any of it."

For once Gabby doesn't seem to have any words and inside I'm giving myself high fives. Quiet boring Jazmine has made loud, extroverted Gabby speechless. I'm on a roll, so I keep going.

"So, where do you go to school now?"

She looks down at the carpet and I have to listen super closely to hear her quiet mutter. "Private school. Half an hour on the bus."

"Have you got any friends? I mean, apart from those girls today?"

She meets my eyes. "Just them."

"Nice?"

She shrugs. "Okay. Not as good as…"

I pounce on her words with a grin. "Not as good as what?"

"Not as good as you, okay?" She makes a face. "Happy now?"

I roll my shoulders. "Happier. Are you going to give me your phone number? I presume you've got a new phone."

Her face clouds over and her shoulders drop. "Why?"

"Why would you not?" My voice is incredulous. "I've just found you again. Why would I want to walk away from my best friend without at least a phone number?"

"I don't do that," she says. "I don't stay in touch with people when I leave."

I sit up straight and hold Wally in my lap. "Well, that's totally stupid," I say, in an imaginary Wally voice, sitting him upright and using his paw as a pointer in Gabby's face. "Very, very dumb."

She looks defensive. "Well, I never have before."

"Did you have friends before?"

She thinks. "Some. Jessie in Year 5. And Daisy in Year 2. They were the ones I liked the best, anyway."

"And you just dropped them?"

She shrugs. Looks away. Then she stands up, stalks over to the window and looks out. "It's just too hard, okay?" But her words are blurred and I can't hear the rest.

"Can you turn around, Gab?" I say. "I can't hear you properly."

She swings towards me, fast, furious; curtains blowing out behind her. The light from the window makes her face dark, but there's a tiny diamond glittering on her cheek.

It's a tear.

"I said it's too hard." Her fists are clenched, mouth is tight. "We pack up, we go, it all starts all over again. And I'm just left."

She stops talking and looks away. "Left on my own."

We're quiet for a moment. I can feel my breath, air in, air out, on my tongue.

"My grandma lives here." My voice is pleading. "I'm going to be coming here during school holidays. Probably a lot because my mum has a boyfriend."

Gabby smiles, even though she probably doesn't want to, with more tears rolling down her cheeks. She looks up at me. "Serious? An actual boyfriend?"

"I know, right?" I look at her with mock horror.

"What's he like? Is he creepy?"

I think for a minute. "Not creepy. Actually, not too bad. I mean, not that I know him yet. But he seems okay." I shake my head. "The whole thing is just, like, weird."

Gabby wipes her eyes with the back of her hand and sniffs loudly. "Give me your phone."

"Why?"

"Duh. I'm going to put my number in it."

I smile. "I'll be here every holidays."

"You'd better."

Grandma's still waiting in the car with Adrian. I have to go. But I have one more question for Gabby.

"I just need to know: what was it like to slap Angela?"

Gabby looks at me like she's holding in the most delicious secret and then she grins bigger than I've ever seen her grin before.

"Totally, completely amazing."

In the car an old Beatles song is playing. It must be classics hour on the radio. Adrian eyes me curiously but Grandma turns to the back seat and says it straight out.

"Things sorted out?"

I nod. My chest is warm inside and I'm sitting straighter than before, taking up more room in my seatbelt. The corners of my mouth keep creeping up on my face, even though I'm deliberately trying to stop from smiling.

"Thanks for taking me."

"Is she happy too?"

"I think so," I say. "We'll probably hang out next time I come here, if that's okay."

Grandma turns back to face the front. I can see a satisfied smile flash between her and Adrian. "That's fine," she says. "Perfect." She reaches down to the volume button and turns up the music and we sing along to Sergeant Pepper's Lonely Hearts Club Band all the way home.

chapter 27

Mum stopped tucking me into bed, like, two years ago, so it's cute that Grandma does it for me, even though I'm nearly fourteen and taller than she is. I like the feeling of being a little kid again, all snuggly in freshly washed pyjamas (thanks Grandma!) and new sheets. At home my doona is light and fluffy and sits on top, but here Grandma uses blankets and tucks everything into the mattress so the bedding feels heavy and tight.

"Goodnight, sweetheart," says Grandma, sitting on the bed beside me.

"Thanks for taking me," I say. "You know, to Gabby's."

She flicks her head like, *hey, no problem*. "Will you be okay?"

"Yeah," I say. "Yeah, I think I will."

She smiles and kisses me and turns the light off and I lie there, all sleepy and weighed down with wool and comfort, and—something I haven't felt in a long time—proud. If I'd brought my journal I would have drawn a picture of me in it with hands in the air, triumphant. A winner. All I wanted to do all night was tell Grandma how I'd talked to Gabby, how I'd fixed the problem, how I'd understood what she was really saying and called her out on it.

For once, when my eyes close, I'm happy. Tonight's dreams will be about flowers and meadows and unicorns and butterflies. I'm sure of it.

I go to sleep.

They are not.

When the first evil green thing shows its face through the trees of the forest I'm apparently hiking in, my stomach jumps with the usual fear, dread and loathing. When the second one peers from a cave, the tip of a knife blade glints in the sunlight and I know that the fantasy is over. I'm on my way again, running and stumbling to find a miracle hiding place where I can keep myself small and silent and wait out the danger and the terror.

'Just go,' I say, grimly, jerking legs and twisting arms and wrists as I hop over rocks, pull myself through trees and slide grassy slopes. 'Just go away and leave me alone,' but my enemies don't stop. I swing my head back to see how close they are and there, only an arm's length behind me are three grinning, green somethings with murder in their eyes.

I put on a burst of speed. The pain of sprinting is bursting, spitting, bruising. My legs are burning, my chest is heaving, my stomach is in my throat. *Get out, get out, get out,* I tell myself, but then it's too late. A hand pulls on my ankle and I'm tripping, falling, tumbling into spiky grass. A thistle gets in my mouth and I spit it out, angry. Above me, the sky is purple and the trees are red and I know without looking that I'm surrounded.

This time they are going to kill me.

I'm marched to a hut in the middle of a clearing and pushed through the wooden door onto a filthy mud floor. Light flashes through tiny holes in the walls and roof and it almost looks pretty. Until I remember how scared I am.

Fear eats me. It starts at my feet, gnaws the strength out of my knees and thighs and travels up to my midsection where it slashes my stomach with a knife, cutting my muscles to ribbons. My arms become playdough and my neck collapses under its hand. I think that I should call for help but when I open my mouth, my voice is frozen.

In the corner, squatting on large, bony feet, is one of my captors, with cruel, bored, almost machine-like eyes that glow in the shadowed light. It's sitting, watching. Biding its time. Letting my own fear kill me off before he finishes the job.

I pull myself into a ball in the opposite corner and watch out of the side of my eye. It's flicking its knife over creepy, claw-like nails, making an irregular cling, clang sound. My neck tightens. The knife seems sharp; bits of nail and claw are flying off, landing on the muddy floor. One piece hits my foot and pricks my skin. Tears creep up to my eyes. They want to escape but I need to keep them in. No need to draw any more attention to myself than necessary.

This always happens, I think to myself. *It's so unfair. They're always trying to get me.*

And then it hits me, rolled up, terrified, pushing back tears.

It's a dream.

It's not real, even though it feels real.

I can choose the ending.

And sometimes I need to fight.

The fear feels like fear, but it's only a dream. It feels like evil is winning, like it's going to kill me, but it's only a dream. The dirt is cool under my fingers; the pinpricks of light are shiny and starry in the darkness; the pain in my legs is stabbing and sharp. But it's all only a dream.

And I can choose the ending.

I stand up, on my fearful, trembling feet. The green thing shakes its head at me in surprise and stands up as well. The blade of its knife is out, pointed towards me.

Time to fight.

Inside I know that I have to kill this evil or it will kill me. There's no doubt. There are no options. The time for running and hiding is over. The time for pleading and begging and hoping and whimpering has passed. Now it is time for me to stand up for myself. Or accept defeat.

And I know something else, something strong and powerful inside me. I don't like defeat.

I step towards the creature. It steps towards me and we circle around the hut, staring each other down, willing the other to lose nerve.

It doesn't speak but I can hear its voice anyway. *You're scared.*

With a still-frozen voice box, I can't speak either, but I can think loudly. *Of course I'm scared.*

You can't do this.

I have to do this.

And I step forward so quickly that I knock it off balance and it falls to its knees on the ground. I kick its hand; the knife skims across the floor to near the door opening. It screams and I yell, voice unfrozen and I dive to pick it up. And then it's me, on my knees, back to the door, knife in hand, threatening it as it scrambles to its feet again.

You can't kill me, it says.

I have to, I say.

There are more of us.

I make a face. *I'll do one at a time.*

My heart is a softball, being thrown again and again at high speed in my chest cavity. The walls seem closer, the ceiling lower. I take a deep breath. Launch myself at my enemy. Aim the knife for its chest. I'm slashing and stabbing with all the strength I can find but its hands are trying to find my neck. It's throwing punches and grasping at my arms but I have to keep going. I'm gagging, heaving, willing myself to keep going. Willing myself to destroy it. To destroy the force that wants to destroy me.

It doesn't die easily. And even at the end, it still kicks and claws, feebly, but with hatred.

There are more of us. It whispers it in a gurgle. Then, finally, its arms and legs fall to the floor, its breathing stops, and its blood forms itself into glistening, stagnant, green-black pools.

I throw myself down so I'm sitting with my back against a wall, panting and crying for breath. *I've killed something.* The words fly around and around my head like manic, attacking magpies. Guilt and terror start to pour in with the light through the cracks in the wall, but I push it back out.

It would have killed me. And I never started this thing.

I know there are two more out there. It's time to finish the job. I creak the wooden door open slowly and peer out into the clearing. No sign of anyone. I back out of the door, pulling the dead creature with me.

Still nothing.

I drag it heavily right out of the hut and dump the body a few metres from the door. It's in full view of the surrounding trees and bushes.

I clear my throat. "Hey," I yell. "You're not going to win. You're not going to destroy me."

There's a rustle of branches and a flock of black cockatoos rise noisily out of the trees. I wait for their cries to subside.

"Come and get me now," I yell, turning to face the opposite direction. "Now's your chance."

But there's nothing. Just a stir and a shake of leaves in the distance and then a still, echoing, silence. And I know, like you *just know* in dreams, that I have won. That no one else will bother me now. That no one is coming after me again. That I can leave here in peace. I put the knife down on my enemy's body, look up to the sky and the light and the birds, watching from far above, and then turn on my heel and walk away.

chapter 28

When my eyes open in the morning sunlight, I'm crying.

Strange. I think to myself. *I'm not sad.* I wipe the wet away with the back of my hand but more and more tears slide down my nose and hit the pillow, creating damp, darkish patches in the pattern of the pillowcase.

Am I leaking?

I swing my legs out of bed, pull on a jacket and head outside to the roses. Grandma is already there with her gloves and tools and bucket. She looks up and her smile quickly turns to concern.

"Good morning Jazmine. Oh. Are you alright?"

My cheeks are wet, my eyes are drippy and my hands are moist from wiping. But for some reason, the tears won't stop.

"I think so," I say.

She stands up quickly, at least, as quickly as an old person with a sprained ankle can stand up. "You need a cup of tea." I don't want to disturb her gardening time but she insists. "A person who wakes up crying needs tea, no question."

She walks me into the house, puts me on the couch

and wraps a throw rug around me so I'm warm. Then she hobbles into the kitchen and puts the kettle on. With the cozy rug and the warm room and the promise of tea, something goes click or bing or some other kind of little noise inside and it's like a traffic light has turned green and all the cars are going at once because the trickle of tears turns into a flood that I can't stop, no matter how many times I wipe my eyes.

Waaaaah.

A sob escapes my chest, pops up into my mouth and lets itself out all over the room.

"Hang on there," yells Grandma. "It's on its way."

She hobbles back in with steaming cups which she puts on the table. Then she throws herself on the couch and sticks her arms out.

"Hug."

It's not a question. I fall into her arms and cry. Quite loudly. And for quite a long time, with all the usual sniffling and snotting and snorting that goes along with it. Because I don't actually feel sad, it's a funny experience. Yes, it's overwhelming and carries me along like a river, tumbling over rocks. But it's also like the tears are scrubbing me clean from the inside. Exfoliating my heart.

And when I finally put my head up and hiccup for the last time, I'm actually peaceful enough to taste, truly savour, every single sip of my tea.

Grandma says nothing the whole time. She's just with me, kind, warm and slurping. It's a strange thing that a person who loves her gourmet food so much would be such a messy tea sipper. I open my mouth to make a joke about it but the words are pushed out of the way by a completely different sentence that forces its way out of my mouth and explodes into the universe.

"Liam is mean to me."

Grandma sits back. She raises her eyebrows. I sit back too, and open my eyes wide.

"I didn't mean to say that," I begin but Grandma stops me.

"Is this the problem you've been having at school?"

I nod. The movement seems easy. Relaxed, even. *Yes. That's the problem.*

"I like him though," I say. But it's not in a defending kind of way, like I'm standing up for him. It's like I've got two objects in my hands and I'm just looking at each of them, wondering how they fit together.

I like him. He's mean to me.

How does that even work?

"Why do you like him?" Grandma asks. Her voice is simple, clear. She's holding her warm cup in her good hand.

I think. It's not hard. "He's funny. He knows sign language."

He also has the most beautiful blue eyes ever in the whole world, I think. But I don't say it out loud.

I add something else on. "And he looks after me."

Grandma's eyebrows go higher.

"And how is he mean to you?"

This one's harder. I mean, I know, kind of. When we're together I end up feeling bad, but then somehow I get to the point of thinking that maybe I'm the mean one, that maybe I'm the one hurting him.

"I'm not really sure," I say, screwing up my face. "I mean, he really likes me. So maybe it's my fault."

Grandma's eyebrows are practically on the ceiling. She brings them down to a normal level.

"Maybe try this," she says. "I'll say something, and you tell me the first two feelings you get when I say it."

I'm curious. "Okay."

She takes in a breath. I wait, suspended and ready.

"Liam," she says.

A rush of grey dread hits my stomach, my back droops and my eyes half close. And then I'm shocked. "How did you do that?" I ask.

She shrugs. "I just said the word. Your body knows how you feel."

"Dread," I say, slowly. "And really, really tired." I shake my head. "That's not good, right?"

Grandma makes a wry face at me.

"Not so much," she says.

"But I like him," I say. "I mean, I really do."

"But?" She lets the question hang in the air and I feel squeamish in the stomach.

"You're saying that because I feel dread and get tired when I think about him, I don't really like him?"

"Not at all," she says. "But if you're feeling that way, there's going to be a reason."

"He's been flirting with Angela," I say, slowly. "And he wants me to always…" I can't finish the sentence.

Grandma looks at me directly. "Always?"

I look down, examine my fingernails. "You know. Do stuff. *That* kind of stuff."

"Do you want to?"

I shake my head. "No. I mean, at least, not yet, right? I'd rather just hang out. And, just so you know, this whole conversation is really embarrassing."

Grandma laughs. "I'm not the one who started it. But seriously. If you say no to, you know, *that stuff*, what happens?"

It's hard to speak. I twist the corner of the rug in my fingers. When I breathe, it's like there's dust in the room. "He says I'm not being fair." And then my voice comes out louder and stronger. "He says I should, that he's waited heaps, and that's what girlfriends do. And then he kind of makes me feel sorry for him, like I'm the one being mean to him, when I just want to have a fun time together without all of that kissing kind of stuff all the time. I still do like him, at least I would if he was like he was at the beginning."

Grandma puts her cup on the table and rubs her hands over her knees a few times.

"People do this sometimes," she says. "They start out really fun and charming and kind. Sometimes it feels like they rescue you out of a bad situation and they do everything to take care of you." She looks at me closely. "And then they start to want you to do everything they want. If you don't, they say you're not being nice, you're not being grateful. But it's not true. It's about control and manipulation. Being in charge of someone rather than loving them."

As she talks, my eyes open wide. "It's just like that," I say. "It's like he wants to control everything I do."

Grandma nods. "And you never quite do it right, and then he makes it into your fault, when actually, he's the one who's not being respectful in the relationship."

I can see it all so clearly, but there's still a nagging feeling, something unexplained at the back of my throat. I take it out, look at it carefully and put it back. It's fear.

"I'm scared though," I say. And now I feel really small and tiny. I can hardly look at Grandma. "Who else is ever going to like me? Liam made me normal."

Grandma's eyebrows are stretched to the curtains on the other side of the room. "Liam made *you* normal? That's a joke, right? You are one of the most likeable, normal, clever, sensitive, thoughtful, pleasant..." she stops for breath, "kind, strong, friendly, loyal people I've ever met."

I'm surprised. But unconvinced. "You have to say that. You're my Grandma."

She makes a face. "There are plenty of people I would *never* say that about, and that includes family members. Believe me, I am telling the absolute, unbiased truth. There are going to be *so many* people who like you, and who love you, in your life. Don't confine yourself to the manipulative loser control-freaks of this world just because you think you're not good enough for anyone else."

She struggles up onto her feet. She's fired up. I'm half-laughing, half-dying from embarrassment.

"Yes, okay, you wear a hearing aid. Big, fat deal. Yes, you've been through some hard times. So have a lot of people. Yes, you're a bit shy sometimes. But you're not abnormal, whatever that means anyway." She throws her hands in the air wildly. "None of that hard stuff means that other people get to boss you around and control you. None of it gives anyone else permission to treat you like rubbish."

She sits back down, puts her hand on my knee and looks straight into my face. "You're allowed to say 'no' if you feel uncomfortable, and no one, not one single person, not Liam, not anyone else, gets to say that you shouldn't. When people start forcing or manipulating or controlling you to do things you don't feel happy doing, they are not your friends. And you should get out of there."

I'm a rush of feelings, bounding and bouncing up out of my heart, knocking each other over as they come pouring out. I'm relieved, confused, amazed and set free, all at the same time, but all I can say is this. "Really?"

"Really." Grandma holds me close.

"I'm so glad you said that."

"I'm glad you told me."

"I'm glad you made me tell you."

She laughs. "I'm glad you let me make you tell me."

I start a sentence but my words get jumbled and I laugh instead.

"What will you do when you get home, do you think?" asks Grandma.

I wait for a minute. "I think I'm going to talk to Liam."

On the drive home Mum and I are mostly quiet, Sunday sport radio grinding away in the background. It's all just white noise for me but I think Mum actually listens to the rugby league occasionally.

"What did you do?" I ask.

She doesn't answer. She seems intent on the footy.

"What did you do?" I ask again.

"Huh?" Her head jerks around. "Do?" She clicks the sound off.

"I mean on the weekend. Did you see Geoff?"

She looks a bit embarrassed. "We went out for dinner. Seafood."

"Oh," I say. I think for a bit. "What did you love?"

She's confused. Frowns. "Love? Do you mean, am I in love?" Her face goes pale.

"No. I mean the food. What did you love on your plate? Grandma always asks me when we go out. 'What did you love?' and I think she wants me to say, 'abalone' or 'buckwheat' or something gross. But I pretty much just can't get past schnitzel. Chicken and breadcrumbs. Yummy."

She laughs. "Maybe you'll love abalone one day."

"Maybe," I say. "Not."

We sit, comfortable for a while longer. I expect Mum to put the radio back on, but she's forgotten about the game. Maybe it's not her team.

"So, it all went okay?" she says, a few minutes later. "With Grandma? The weekend."

I nod.

"School tomorrow? Not going to stay home?"

I shake my head. "School tomorrow."

She shoots a half glance out of the side of her eyes like she's wondering if she should ask or pry or find out the things mothers are supposed to find out but she obviously decides it might be risky because she turns back to watch the road and lets her fingers find the volume button. We drive home listening to the Rabbitohs thrash the Bulldogs and the distant static of crowds cheering.

When we pull up in our driveway I take in a deep breath and let it out noisily.

"Home," says Mum. "Can you grab your bag?"

"Okay."

Mum's halfway up the steps with her key out, ready to unlock the door while I'm still pulling the bag out of the back. I stop her with my voice.

"Mum."

She turns. Looks at me, expectantly.

"Are you?"

She narrows her eyes, waiting. "Am I what?"

"In love. With Geoff."

She swallows, fingers jingle the keys. Her mouth twists sideways. "Just get the bag. Come on, let's go. I've got to get dinner on."

Inside, my room is the same as it always was. Blue doona cover, white bookcase, hammock chair and the fake wood desk Mum inherited from her work. I'm home. But it's different. Can you grow up in just one weekend? Because somehow I feel older, all in one hit. Like everything is smaller now. Or I'm looking at it with different eyes. Or something.

I sit on the bed and stretch my fingers over the fuzzy throw Mum bought me when I was 10. It's draped half over the drawer in my bedside table where I keep my phone but I'm nervous to move it. I don't want to get my phone out and see what's in it. Messages from Liam. Or maybe, no messages from Liam. I can't decide which would be worse.

Don't look, I decide. *Don't even peek. Just focus. You know what you need to do tomorrow.*

I drape the throw over the drawer, pile books on it and then go outside to pull weeds. No temptation.

At night, I'm wary of going to sleep. I lie awake and read books and science project information sheets. Anything to keep my mind off tomorrow and the conversation I'm going to have to have. The question I'm going to have to ask. I can't quite believe it when my eyes open at sunrise and I realise two things. First, I wasn't awake all night. Second, no bad dreams.

Yes, I stood in the same clearing as the night before but the hut had gone. Grass and wild flowers had sprung up, hiding any sign that anything had ever been there. Also gone was anything that wanted to chase me.

"Hello?" I said out loud to the trees but the only answer was the breeze in my hair.

chapter 29

This morning I'm calm on the inside. There's a deep, quiet stillness at my centre. But it's not quite making it to the outside of me. When I'm on the bus, a tiny electric current runs and zips in my toes. As I get closer to school it gets stronger, zapping my legs and knees and moving up to my stomach and down into my hands. When we pull up I can hardly pick up my bag for twitchy fingers.

"Aveagooday," says the bus driver, and I throw him a half smile and step down onto the concrete, breathing sharp and short up in my chest. I can't see Liam yet. The crowd of kids is thick and noisy and I'm swinging my head around wildly. If he's not here, what will I do? I'm all prepared for this moment, this conversation, this time. Will I have to rethink it all? Psyche myself up all over again?

But it's okay. I feel him before I see him. It's a tap on the shoulder and a touch on my back and then I hear his voice.

"Jaz. You're here."

I swing around. He's smiling at me, blue eyes clear and sunny and for a second I melt all over again. *What was I worried about?*

"Where have you been? Two days away. And all weekend. And I sent you like 25 texts which you didn't even answer," he says. His mouth goes from a smile to a half pout. Around us, the swarm of school uniforms is thinning, dribbling through the gate and down the path towards school.

"Sick," I say. The lie pops out without even a pause for thought but it kicks me as it leaves my mouth. *Tell the truth.* "And then I went to my Grandma's."

"Missed you," he says. He drops his bag and takes both my hands. "Missed you a lot." He looks at me meaningfully and moves in closer.

Remember what you're doing.

I pull one hand away. Chew my lip.

"Um. I have to ask you a question."

"What?" He goes to grab my hand back. I flip it away and for a second we look like we're doing some kind of funny dance. I'm confused and then I find my strong centre again. Stand straight.

"The twins told me something about you." I look at his eyes, searching. "Something you did? At a party. With Angela."

There's a tiny flash of anger across his face. It's not big. It probably wouldn't be obvious to anyone else, but I can see it. I know what it is. "What party? What am I supposed to have done?" He changes his face and holds out his arms. "Forget it. Hug? Come on."

I don't move. "In the holidays." There's a calm, clear feeling across my chest. "They say you guys were getting with each other."

Fear in his eyes. And then annoyance.

"That's stupid," he says. "They have no right to say that."

"I just want to know if it's true."

"Why would you even ask a question like that?" His voice is higher. More intense. A couple of girls hanging around raise their heads in interest, but their friends pull them away and then it's just him and me, on the concrete, beside the high metal gates. "Are you, like, jealous or something? Don't you trust me? I'm really hurt that you would even think Caitlin and Olivia are telling the truth. Everyone knows they just spread rumours. They're like Stupidum and Stupidee. Angela's right about them."

I frown. "What does Angela say about them?"

He's angry, suddenly. "Why do you want to know? Forget it. It doesn't matter. Think about what's important. You're accusing me of cheating. That's not cool, Jaz. Not cool at all."

"I'm not accusing you." I try to keep my voice steady.

"Sounds like you're accusing me. Sounds like, 'waah, Liam, you're such a cheater, such a bad guy, waah'."

"I didn't say any of those things." From the corner of my eye I see the last bus pull away. *Keep it together. Stay calm.*

"You didn't need to. I knew what you meant. And I can't believe you'd think that of me." His face goes melty and gorgeous again. "I've always looked after you. I'm your boyfriend, right?" His blue eyes are pleading.

I can feel my heart getting pulled along, back to the place where I ask nothing and get no answers. I shut my eyes for a second. Break the spell.

"I just asked a question. That's all." My voice is a hint

louder.

"You don't have to shout." He takes a step back. Looks hurt. "Don't yell at me."

"I'm not yelling." I finger the strap of my bag nervously. "I just want to know if it's true."

"If what's true? If I'm apparently a cheater, and Caitlin and Olivia, the biggest you-know-what's of the school are making up rubbish?"

I'm shocked. Hurt. "Don't call my friends—our friends—that."

"Just saying it like it is. You want me to be honest, right? Since the party those two have been such losers. Total gossips. They just tell lies."

Now I'm mad. But I have to stay focused.

"You're changing the subject." I grit my teeth. "Can you please. Just. Tell me. Did you and Angela kiss at the party?"

"Jaz," he says. "Jaz, Jaz, Jaz," and he tilts his head to the side like Dad did the time when I was four and I drew a picture of Mum and me as princesses on the wall in the lounge room. Dad was disappointed. But also amused.

I lift my chin. Four year olds can win arguments too. "Well, did you?"

His face goes black. "Stop pushing me. You're being really mean."

"I'm not."

"You're nagging and hassling me."

"I'm just asking."

"Stop asking."

I stamp my foot. Forget calm. Forget focused. The yell comes up from my stomach, furious and strong.

"No. I won't stop asking." There's an edge of a scream in my voice. "It's a simple question. Yes or no. Did you and Angela kiss at the party?"

And then it's like the world is spinning slower. Two seconds seem to be drawn out to ten. And I'm watching what happens from inside myself, standing on the sidelines, a few steps back. In slow motion, Liam's fists clench. His chin lifts. And then he steps heavily towards me, raising his arms. A breath pushes out of me, awkward and shocked and my feet step back and away, my body caving in on itself in fear.

Thud, thud, pause, thud thud, pause.

My heart beats in my ears. From somewhere behind my eyes, I'm looking out at my boyfriend, the one who said he'd always look after me, raising his fists, ready to hurt me.

And then it comes to me. I know where I am. I know what this is.

I can choose the ending.

Time to fight.

I uncurl from my corner and step out, arms crossed. Taking up space. Breathing fierce. And I see something I've never seen before. Liam's eyes blink, his hands fall and his shoulders drop. And he steps back.

"Just tell me," I say. And my voice is as calm and as strong as I've ever heard it, like a teacher who expects to be listened to, like a young child who's never heard the word 'no'.

Liam looks away. He's small, like a little boy.

"What if I did?" he says. His voice is whiny. "It's hardly my fault. Angela came on to me and you weren't there and anyway, you hardly gave me anything for weeks before that. All you wanted to do was hold hands which was, like, so, I don't know, so young! I mean, if you're not going to, you can hardly blame me for getting with Angela."

When the twins first told me, I'd been shaky. Upset. Devastated. But now it's different. Hearing the truth from Liam's own mouth makes me calm. Decided.

"I want to break up."

"What?" He looks like he can't believe what he's hearing.

"With you." I'm firm and strong. "I don't want to be your girlfriend anymore."

"Just because some girl came on to me and I made a little mistake—yeah, okay, I'll admit it—it was a mistake." He sounds indignant.

"We won't hang around together any more, okay?" I say. I try to move away, but he grabs my hand and doesn't let go.

"Jazmine. I'm really, really sorry. I made a mistake. I apologise. What more do you want me to say?" He sounds desperate and I almost feel sorry for him. Almost.

"I don't want to go out with someone who cheats," I say. "I just don't."

"But it wasn't my fault." He's nearly crying.

In my head, I have a picture of me hugging him, saying *it's okay, it's okay, I didn't want to make you feel bad,* and him sniffling and apologising. I look at it for a half second, consider it. In the picture, I put out my other hand to him and he grabs it. So far so good. But then he pulls me closer and moves in to get to my mouth and immediately I feel bad again.

Uncomfortable.

Out of my depth.

Used.

I shake my head. "It was your fault. You could have said no." I pull my hand out of his, feeling the sweat and the skin and the cling of the ownership he's had over me for so many months, and I begin to walk away.

"Please don't," he says. "Please?"

I turn back. "I actually like you, Liam. At least, I did. But I can't be with someone who treats me badly."

His face turns hard. "You won't be with anyone then," he says. He spits the words out. "I did you a favour, asking you out. And having you in our group. Everyone was like, 'really, her? The deaf girl?' when I first started to hang out with you. You won't have anyone, you know."

A cold shake goes through me. One part of my head is screaming. *It's true. Say sorry. Take what you're given.* But the other part, the strong part who knows now that she can climb a mountain and rescue her grandmother; the part who's sick of the hassle, who's strong enough now, shakes her head. She's not upset. She's just bored. *You're fine,* she says to me. *You'll be fine. Walk away.*

I make a little face. "I think I'll take my chances," I say and head up the path.

"Caitlin and Olivia are scrags," he yells after me. "And so are you. You're going to regret this."

I turn back.

"I've dealt with worse," I say. And I smile. Because I have. And I've survived.

And I know I don't need to go back.

chapter 30

I do, however, need to go to the nearest bathroom.

I'm okay walking up the path while Liam is watching me. My legs work fine. My breathing is normal. But as soon as I'm out of his sight everything kind of falls apart. My bones seem to disconnect and to even keep my bag on my shoulder I have to think about which fingers are holding it and how they're connected to my arm and my shoulder and my back. I'm taking jerky steps, kicking my feet out in front of me and making little chest noises that I can't control.

Urrugmph. Eehh.

Time to find cover.

I head to the girls' toilets, slide into a booth and collapse onto a toilet seat.

Did I just…?

Yes. I did.

I wait for the tears to come, for the rush of emotion, the great moment of 'aaaaahhhh' you get when everything just falls out of you. But there's no prickle of wet, no welling up or spilling out. Nothing.

Okaaaay, I say to myself. *Surprising. But not bad.*

I'm blinking a little. Half smiling. Just waiting to see what's going to happen, but there's still no big outpouring. No overwhelming reactions.

Instead, it's just a quiet feeling of peace. I hold my hand up to my heart.

I break up with my boyfriend, and it feels like this?

I can hardly believe it. I wriggle my fingers and toes. Everything seems to be reconnected. My feet try out a few steps. They can walk. Everything works like it should, and I feel fine. I put a picture of Maths, my first class of the day, into my head, just to see what the reaction is. There's a bit of nervousness as I imagine finding a seat and telling the teacher where I've been, but when I think about looking over and seeing Liam sitting with Angela, I actually feel okay.

So, I guess I'll go then, I tell myself in the mirror and give myself an experimental thumbs up. But just as I'm heading through the door and about to turn the corner out onto the path, I can hear faint crying and fast footsteps and then, *bam,* I'm bumped out of the way by a bag and a plait and a girl, no, two girls, who are heading straight into the bathrooms I've just come out of.

I shake myself. Focus my eyes. "Olivia? Caitlin?"

One of the crying, running dervishes stops and whirls around. "Jazmine?" she says.

The other one turns around as well. "Is is true?"

"Is what true?" I ask.

"That Liam broke up with you?" says Caitlin. Her face is white, voice broken with tears. "We heard it from Dan just now."

"Is that what he's saying?" My eyebrows are high. A laugh escapes from my stomach. "Wow." I shake my head. "Just, wow."

"Did he?" asks Olivia. Her eyes are huge. Saucers on her face.

"We broke up," I say. "But he didn't break up with me."

Olivia's eyes are dinner plates. Caitlin's face is even paler than before. "Really? So it's not true, then."

"What's not true?"

"That you cheated on him." She says it in such a tiny, breathless voice that I can hardly hear her.

Now I have to laugh out loud. "Seriously? That's what he's saying? That's ridiculous."

"You should go and tell everyone it's not true," says Olivia. Her lip is quivering. "You don't want rumours like that to go around."

For a second I think, *yeah, she's right* and the beginning of a rage of injustice rises up from my toes but it only gets to about my knees before I see it for what it is: totally nuts.

"You know what?" I say, and I shrug, a big one, right up to my ears. "Who cares? He wants to spread stories, so what? I know it's not true. And I'd rather just get on with my life."

Caitlin drops her bag. Her whole body is incredulous. "But... what life? Haven't you heard? They're chucking you, *us*, out of the group."

Olivia nods furiously and then dissolves into tears. "We're getting..."

They say it together. "Shunned."

I lift my eyebrows. "Really? They're throwing you out too?" And for a moment, I am angry. Not for myself, but because no one should hurt the twins. They don't deserve it. "I'm really sorry."

Olivia's blubbing now, pouring out tears and hiccupping big sobs. "I mean, I expect Angela to be mean, but I never thought Erin and Liam would be so…"

"… vicious," finishes Caitlin. She's wiping her eyes, slumped against the sink. "We've been friends since primary school."

"That's harsh." I slide down next to her and without even thinking put my arm around her. "You'll be okay."

She lays her head on my shoulder and has another little cry. "Thanks."

I hold out both arms to Olivia who comes in for a hug as well. She's practically dripping, she's been crying so much. We sit there together for a few minutes while they snuffle and hiccup and burst out into extra little crying episodes, apparently randomly. Finally, they seem to be finished and I pat them on the shoulders and stand up. My legs need a stretch.

"You don't seem upset, Jaz," says Caitlin, after she's pulled about 25 pieces of tissue paper out of the dispenser and used each one to wipe up her snot and tears.

"I know," I say, and I sound as amazed as she does. "But I'm really not." I pull away and face them. "It's even kind of the opposite."

"Why?" Caitlin looks shocked. Scandalized.

"Well, it's weird. But it's kind of like an adventure," I say. My voice goes up in excitement. "I mean, if you think about it, do you even *like* Angela?"

Olivia looks up at me and shakes her head.

"No," ventures Caitlin.

"Do you like sitting with her and all those stupid girls?" I ask.

The twins look at each other.

"Me either," I say. "And I'm the one who broke up with Liam, so it's not as if I want to hang around them any more." I look out through the door to the quadrangle. "We can do anything. We can sit with anyone if we want to." I turn back to the twins, willing them to see what I can see. "We're free."

There's a silence. I can see a tap dripping out of the corner of my eye. It's like the ticking hand of a classroom clock, punctuating the seconds. I can see Olivia and Caitlin's brains thinking. Freedom's a new concept for them, like it is for me. But they haven't had time to get used to it like I have.

"What do you guys want to do?" I ask. "Do we have a plan?"

"Well, we have to go to class when the bell goes," says Caitlin, always the practical one.

"Yeah. It's Science next," says Olivia. Her face is still streaky.

"Science," I say. It brings a grin to my face. "Alvin and the Chipmunks. Girls, I think I know what our plan is going to be."

And that's what it is. We clean up and we chat and we hug and say how stupid Angela is—and Liam too—for a while and then I get sick of talking about them so I say we shouldn't bother with them, we should just talk about ourselves, so we do. I tell them all about finding Gabby again and why she left like she did and we hug again and resolve that we'll never fight, that we'll always tell each other the truth, and we'll always stick close. And then, when the bell goes, we pick up ourselves and our bags and we head out, the three of us with our shoulders together, to Science. Alvin and Seb and Cammo are waiting to tell me all about the research and the work they've done on the project, and I introduce them to the twins properly and then we have recess together and then lunch, later.

And all day I feel lighter.

Liam glowers at me from across the room in English and also in Drama but you know what? I don't really care. Because I was right. I've dealt with worse, and I don't need his hassle. He tries for two weeks or so to get at me; first it's just looks, and then I start to hear stories about stuff I've done or not done, and then he tries actually sending messages with Dan and Erin, directly to me, saying he misses me and he loves me. I know it's to try to get me back, but I haven't missed feeling bad and scared and out of my depth. Not one speck. And I certainly don't want to go back. So I ignore it all and ignore him and ignore the evil glances Angela shoots at me as well because I know I'm stronger than her.

And I sleep well.

At night, I have dreams, but no one's chasing me. No one is threatening me. No one's trying to kill me. They're just normal dreams. The sort that makes you think, 'hey, that was random,' in the morning, if you can even remember it. And that's when I wake: in the morning. Not in the middle of the night. It's morning when I open my eyes. Morning when I go out to the garden. Morning when I check my messages (usually, at least one from Gabby, and recently, quite a few from Alvin. He manages to find at least two really important things to tell me about the project every single day.) It's also morning when I go out to the kitchen and see Mum.

"Want breakfast?" she says, every day.

"I'll make it for you," I say and I open the fridge and pull out the muesli I've been soaking (Grandma's recipe) or the rolls I've made (also Grandma's recipe). I cook and prepare while she watches and then we eat.

"What do you love?" I ask her, every time.

"Definitely the pumpkin seeds," she says today, pulling one out of her muesli.

"Really?"

"Mmm. No. Not really. But they're healthy, aren't they?" She smiles. "I probably *should* love them."

"I love the blueberries," I say. And I mean it. Grandma has a punnet of blueberries in her fridge the whole time. I've got plans to put a blueberry bush in my garden and make her my blueberry muffins next time I visit. Maybe share one with Gabby too.

"Can I go down to Grandma's this weekend? I mean, if she wants me," I ask. "Are you busy with Geoff?"

Mum lifts her head and bites her lip. "I'd like to see him, of course."

I put my spoon down on the table. Take a breath. "So, maybe he could come too. Get Grandma to invite Adrian. We could go for a hike now that her ankle's working again."

Mum's quiet for a minute. "You wouldn't mind?"

I wait and then shake my head. *No. I don't mind.*

I can see her fingers moving. "It could work." She tips her head to one side, like, *we could try it.*

I stand up, take my bowl to the sink. Time to get dressed for school. As I'm just about to shut my door I stick my head back out.

"Hey, Mum."

She looks around from her chair at the table. She's cradling her cup of tea.

"You know that question I asked you? Ages ago."

"Which one?"

"The one about Geoff. And love."

She's quiet.

"I want to know."

"Why?"

"I just do."

Mum looks at her hands. She takes a deep breath. "So ask it."

"Are you in love with Geoff?"

She stops a beat, looks at the table. And then speaks. "Yes, Jazmine. I think I probably am."

I'm silent. I close the door to my room, look around for my clothes, but I can't find anything for the blur in front of my eyes. I open my journal and pick up a pen, but I can't write anything. The ceiling above me is as blank as the paper in front of me. I'm not sad or upset. I'm not angry. I'm not even happy or excited. I'm everything, and nothing, all together and all at once. Then, my pen finds the page and I'm drawing, but it's not what I expect. Somehow, a sketch of Trembler's Rocks is emerging from my hand, with the boulders and the sheer scale of the cliffs and the view out to the harbour and the ocean.

I look at it. And then I add a boat, the tiny little *Invincible*. And then I put me in it, navigating out of the harbour, right into the open sea.

My stomach goes wobbly, and then, just as suddenly, calm and strong, and underneath I write these words:

He's not my dad.

That's okay.

I put the pen down and I know, somehow, that I don't have to solve it all today, this minute, this hour. That I don't have to hide from it or live in fear. Just launch. And sail. See where the wind blows and where the ocean goes. And weather the storms.

I get dressed and pack my bag with books, pens and my phone. I do my hair, put on some mascara. And then I walk out of my room, through the kitchen and up the hall to Mum's room, where she's sitting on her bed, looking almost as dazed as I was. I sit down beside her and hug her. She looks surprised. In a good way.

"What's that for?" she says.

I shrug. "No reason," I say. "I just love you."

She hugs me back, solid and rich. "School now?"

"I'm ready," I say, but before I leave the room and open the door to the sunshine I look at her face. She's smiling.

And so am I.

acknowledgements

I wasn't ever going to write a sequel to Invisible. It seemed to me that I'd said everything I could say about Jazmine and I had no idea what could possibly happen to her next. But then I had letters from the fans who kept wanting to know what was coming next for her. *Would there be a sequel? Pleeeeease?*

I caved in.

And I'm glad I did. It was fun to go back into Jazmine's world and help her grow and change even more. To anyone who was unhappy with how Liam turned out, I'm sorry. The inspiration for his manipulative streak came from Madeleine Kim who told me she thought Liam was just TOO perfect.

"No one's really like that," she said.

She was probably right. Of course, not everyone's as mean as Liam is, either. But, girls! Choose your partners wisely, and don't be afraid to stand up for yourselves.

So, thank you to the fans who inspired the book, the lovely 'likers' on Facebook who kept telling me they were interested in my progress, and to the Jazmine-followers who were always interested in what came next.

Thank you also to my kind and generous band of readers who gave me useful feedback on the finished draft; Linda T, Heather Y, Kerrie A, Penny M, Heaven A, Joana H, Aniruddh, Erin K, Kyla L and the inimitable Katie J Cross, author of the 'Miss Mabel's School for Girls' series. My writing group colleagues, Selena, Colleen and Bruce, have made me a better writer in the short time I've been with them and I'm grateful. Amanda C picked up some errors in her reading and was so helpful to email them through. I'll have to hire her next time!

I'm also appreciative of this generous band of people who supported my writing by putting their money where their mouths were: Tracey Hall, Karen Grundy, Caroline Hill, Tracey Reynolds, Sue Davies, Bruno and Elizabeth Henke, Cathy Barker, Pauline Egan, Nick Parish, Rachel Farley, Katherine Seers, Selena Hanet-Hutchins, Jean Boer, Michael and Jess Winkler, Cameron Ellis, Penny Morrison, Lina Mendez, Dee Kelley, Sophie Blanc, the lovely ladies from the corner shop, Marie, Linda, Irene and Judy, Vicki Craig, Pam Tow, Paula and Mick from the Kangaroo Valley Fudge Shop, Linda Chittick, Kathy Crawshaw, Katie Cross, Joanna Arnold, Rick Chen, Eunice Hill, Rosie Sutton, Lisa O'Neill, Sharon Andrews, Ellise Barkley, Ingrid McPhail, Karen Barker, Kristen Young, Nancy Curry, Catherine Nash, Mariette Wray, Hannah Boland, Sarah Bull, Jannah Walton, Ann Knox-Gillan, George Athas, Brenda Sambrook, Janet Harrison, Fleur Creighton, Annie Bartholomeusz, Ellie Bennetts, Lauren Avery and Laura Nelson.

Being a terrible organiser, it is very, very likely I have left someone off this list, so if you think you should be on here, for any reason whatsoever, please insert your name. It has been omitted solely due to incompetence on my part!

As always I need to thank my husband who generously provides me with time and freedom to write.

And I must thank you, the readers and fans, who write to me and let me know just how special Jazmine has been for you. You make it all worthwhile.

also by Cecily Anne Paterson

Invisible

Book 1 in the Invisible Series
The first story about Jazmine, Invisible was a semi-finalist in the
Amazon Breakthrough Novel Award 2014.

Being Jazmine

Book 3 in the Invisible Series
When you don't know where you belong, who are you really?
Jazmine's deaf. And she's tired. Tired of trying hard, tired of pretending
to be like everyone else. When Jaz goes to deaf camp, a new world
opens up to her. But when you leave one world and enter another, what
happens to the people you leave behind?

The Coco and Charlie Franks Series

Two books, Love and Muddy Puddles, and its sequel, Charlie Franks is
A-OK, follow the Franks twins from the city after their father moves the
whole family to the country in an attempt to bond. For readers 11-13.

The Kangaroo Valley School Series

Three books all about friendship, popularity, finding your voice and
following your dreams, set in Year 6 at the tiny Kangaroo Valley Village
school. Great for readers 9-12.

stay in touch

If you liked this story, I'd love to let you know
when my new books are coming out. Sign up at
www.cecilypaterson.com/intheloop and I'll send you
a newsletter full of awesome reading suggestions for
brave hearted girls every month, plus some offers on
how to get more of my books for free.

Connect with me at all these places:
Website: www.cecilypaterson.com
Facebook: www.facebook.com/CecilyAnnePaterson/
Insta: www.instagram.com/cecilypaterson/
Twitter: @CecilyPaterson